the next full moon

Downtown Bookworks Inc.
285 West Broadway, New York, New York 10013
www.downtownbookworks.com

CAROLYN TURGEON

the next full moon

downtown bookworks

DEDICATION

To my mother, father and sister

ACKNOWLEDGMENTS

This book would never have come into being if not for Julie Merberg asking to me to write something for her new children's book publishing company while I was Skyping with her gorgeous family from Berlin, Germany (while they were in Berlin, New York) one autumn afternoon a couple of years ago. I am eternally grateful to Julie for this, and to her brilliant husband, my good friend David Bar Katz, and their wild, beautiful, mop-headed boys Morris, Nathaneal, Kal, and Mac, who were all so much a part of this process. Thank you, too, to everyone else at Downtown Bookworks, especially to Patty, Georgia, and Sarah, as well as to everyone at Simon & Schuster. It's a wonderful thing, when someone offers you the chance to go back in time and be twelve again.

I WOULD ALSO LIKE TO THANK

My agent Elaine Markson and her fabulous right-hand assistant Gary Johnson.

Miss Hannah Kurtz, who sat down one day and told me all about the secret lives of adolescents.

Hannah Stout, who's in love with all insects but with mayflies in particular and made me (kind of) love them, too.

Olivier Georgeon, who discussed this book with me endlessly and suggested, in his French and scientific manner, that budding swan maidens would shed their robes.

My uncle, John Krinbill, who took me to a city full of swans.

Max Spiegel, Chantelle Hodge, and Jim Downes, who all generously taught me about fly fishing.

Eric Schnall, Jeanine Cummins, Laura Carleton, Mary McMyne, and Valerie Cates, all of whom read early drafts of this book.

Jill Gleeson, who was there with me as I finished this book, in a 12-hour writing session at an unglamorous fast food chain, and endured me reading pages and pages of it out loud to her over the course of that day and several others.

My sister, Catherine, and parents, Alfred and Jean, for being so supportive and generally being the best family ever.

And, finally, I'd like to thank the real Jeff Jackson, who was the most popular boy in the 7th grade when I went to MacDonald Middle School in East Lansing, Michigan in 1983. I don't think I ever actually spoke to him, but you really never forget your first crush.

Love, Carolyn

CHAPTER ONE

*I*t started with a feather. One little white rounded feather resting on her pillow. Ava didn't think much of it, though, considering that it was a bright Sunday morning and there were only three weeks left of school and in just over a month she would turn thirteen and the whole summer stretched out before her like a long, shimmering gift. She jumped out of bed, letting the feather blow to the ground, where it landed on the dark wood floor and, after skittering a few inches in the faint breeze, came to a stop. Any passerby might have thought it was a bit of fur and indeed the cat, Monique, eyed it suspiciously as she slinked past Ava's room and to the kitchen.

Ava stepped over it as she rushed to her bathroom, to the big mirror. She'd spent the day before lying in the backyard on a towel and hoped that for once her skin might have turned tan and smooth, like Jennifer Halverson's, who, with her sun-drenched blond hair and brown skin, looked like she spent her whole life at the beach even though she lived right smack in the middle of Pennsylvania like the rest of them. Ava half expected to have turned blond and dark-skinned herself overnight, but there she was, staring back at herself, the same as ever. Pale, though now more pink than white, and dark-haired, with navy blue eyes. Boring. She sighed and turned away.

Ava Gardner looks, her grandmother called them. *Like the old-time movie star. Women used to walk around with umbrellas to have skin as beautiful as yours.* Ava would roll her eyes. "That was like a thousand years ago," she'd say. When she looked in the mirror, it was like a ghost girl looking out.

But this morning was too beautiful for a little paleness to ruin it. Summer was almost here! The windows were wide open and the air smelled like grass and flowers and trees. The white curtains on her windows fluttered in the breeze, which felt warm and wonderful against her skin. Not too hot, just warm enough.

She clicked on her computer and saw that Morgan was already on IM. "Ready to go?" she typed. "We can work on our tans before anyone else gets there."

"Sure," MORGANISAWESOME typed back. "Come'n get me."

THE NEXT FULL MOON

"Be there in 10."

Ava pulled off her nightshirt and shimmied into her new bathing suit, which she'd been saving. It was the first day her friends and classmates would be going to the lake, where they'd spend the rest of the summer hanging out, day after long blissful day. Ava loved it down there: the trees hanging over the water, the canoes and paddleboats whirring in the distance, the long line of beach, and of course the old carousel next to the stands selling flavored ice and lemonade. She could hardly wait. And she knew that Jeff Jackson would be there—she'd heard him and all his friends planning it the week before.

Even thinking about him here, alone in her room, made her blush.

She wondered what Jeff would think when he saw her in her new suit. Nervously, she examined herself in the mirror, twisting this way and that, worrying that he'd think her stomach wasn't flat enough, that her thighs were too big. She had to admit that the suit looked good on her, that the red was striking against her long dark hair.

Lately, she was sure that Jeff had started noticing her. He'd smiled at her in the hallway last week, and she hadn't been able to focus on anything for hours after. But of course she was far too shy to talk to him. In her imagination, though, she'd smiled back and leaned on a locker alluringly. "Going to the lake this weekend?" she'd asked, giving him a wink.

"Maybe I'll see you there."

Now she shook her head and pulled on some shorts and a T-shirt, grabbed her bag and some flip-flops. She should be a little more brave, she thought. After all, she was about to be a teenager.

"Dad, I'm ready!" she called out, rushing to the kitchen to grab a banana and a granola bar.

No answer.

"Dad!"

Monique stood by the kitchen window and even she ignored Ava, glancing over her shoulder once and then turning back to the hummingbird fluttering about the birdfeeder outside.

Ava rolled her eyes and stomped down to the basement. Her father would be in his workroom, of course. If he wasn't teaching or out in the creek fishing, he was there. She couldn't understand how he could pass hours happily sitting in one spot, making bamboo fishing rods by hand. But he loved it—working with wood, putting together rods and lures that he'd give away or use to fish in the creek. They didn't even eat the fish he caught! Her dad could spend all day catching fish after fish and then tossing them back into the water. What was the point?

Crazy.

"Dad!"

She rushed down the stairs. Loud jazz was playing behind his shut door. She banged on it, then pushed in.

"Dad!"

His head shot up in surprise, and he looked even more out of sorts than ever, with his wild salt-and-pepper hair and crooked glasses, a mess of bamboo spread out in front of him on the table. The room smelled like wood and varnish.

"Are you trying to give your dad a heart attack?" he asked.

"Your music was on. And you promised to take me and Morgan to the lake."

"What time is it?"

"Ten a.m. The sun is shining, and I should be outside. So should you!"

"Ten already, huh?" He sighed and grabbed the car keys lying on the table. As he stood, his hand reached out to grab something floating down in the air.

"What's this?" he asked. He opened his palm. One white feather with blood on the tip. He looked at it and then up at her, his face suddenly worried.

Ava shrugged. "How would I know? You're the one who spends your whole life down here in the dark. Come on, Dad, we're late!"

"Okay, okay," he said, placing the feather on the table and turning to the door. "Let's go, earlybird."

Her heart pounded with excitement as they drove to Morgan's house. Morgan was waiting outside, her bright pink towel rolled up and sticking out of her tote bag. She ran down to the car, all long red hair and freckles and gangling legs and arms, and bounced into the backseat.

Morgan was Ava's best friend, even though she could be embarrassing with her loud laugh and sometimes—well, oftentimes—spastic behavior. But they had been best friends since nursery school and there was no turning back now. Plus, Morgan was the funniest girl in school.

The drive to the lake was beautiful, as they left their little college town and headed into the countryside, where the roads turned narrow and winding and everything was bright green and charming little cabins popped up on the side of the road. They crossed mountains that looked over entire valleys coated in a morning mist. Finally, they turned down the gravel lane that led into the lake parking lot.

The girls gathered their things and Ava assured her father that she'd be home by dinnertime, that Morgan's mother would be picking them up in the afternoon.

"What are you doing today, Dad?" she asked, feeling suddenly guilty for leaving him alone. He was alone so often.

"I think I might head to the creek, do some fishing," he said. "Get a little sun." He made a face at her.

"Maybe you should go out with some friends or something," she said. "I hear some people actually like that kind of thing. Friends and stuff."

"Ha ha. Now off with you both."

Ava watched after him as he drove away and then she and Morgan rushed down to the lake. She tried to walk as calmly as she could, aware at every moment that Jeff could be there already. She scanned the beach, which was not yet full of people the way she knew it would be later. She and Morgan were the first ones there from their school. A smattering of other people were setting out towels and picnic baskets.

They set down their bags and towels in a prime spot, close to the water, and stripped down to their bathing suits.

As Ava started rubbing herself with tanning lotion, Morgan pulled out a huge pair of pink, heart-shaped sunglasses and put them on. "I'm sorry, my friend, but you are glowing," she said.

"I laid out yesterday."

"You're supposed to lay out in the *sun*, dummy."

"I *did*, you dork. And look how white you are, too."

"I'm a redhead, I'm supposed to be the color of porcelain. Like Nicole Kidman."

"Whatever. Your glasses are stupid. They clash with your hair."

"Stupid awesome, maybe."

Ava sighed loudly and lay back on the towel. "Well. Don't come crying to me when you get heart-shaped tan lines on your face."

They both broke into giggles. The sun beat down, already making them sweat.

"I wish it could stay summer forever," Morgan said, after a few minutes.

"Me, too."

"Let's move to California."

"Okay. We can be movie stars there."

"And have a pool."

"And a convertible."

Ava closed her eyes and pictured the two of them riding around in a convertible with scarves around their necks, blowing kisses as people waved at them from the streets. Jennifer Halverson would come running up for an autograph and Ava would push down her sunglasses and ask, "Do I know you?" Of course Jeff Jackson would be in the car with them and he wouldn't remember her either.

"Let's swim a little," Morgan said, after a while.

"Okay," Ava answered, reluctantly coming out of her reverie. The beach was much more crowded now. Towels and bodies were spread out in every direction.

They headed to the water, and Ava broke into a run. She never felt more happy or free than she did here. It was summer, finally! The lake was a dark, beautiful blue. Morgan dashed ahead of her.

"It's freezing!" Morgan called as she plunked her foot into the lake.

Ava didn't care. The cold never bothered her. She dove straight in, and, as always, it was like entering another world.

All the sounds went mute, the smells went away, and the world turned hushed and dark. She smiled into the water as she pushed forward. Twisting around, moving onto her back and her sides, coming up for air and then pushing back under. There were people all around and yet she couldn't have felt more alone than she did then. But in the best possible way.

She pushed her head above water again and swam out to the buoys. In the distance, a line of trees, like fringe, reached up to the sky.

And then behind her, laughter.

She turned.

Morgan was standing in the water laughing, talking to him. Jeff Jackson. Tall and manly. Well, maybe not manly, but surely the only boy in seventh grade who was almost as tall as her father, with broad shoulders, a dimpled chin, and bright blond hair.

He caught her eye and without thinking she immediately ducked her head underwater. Wishing she could hide away.

Then she realized how stupid she looked.

She wanted to disappear at the bottom of the lake. Why did she always have to be so dorky? Why couldn't she act like the girl in her fantasies?

She squeezed her eyes shut and played a movie in her head of what she should have done: smiled at him elegantly, tossing her hair like Jennifer Halverson was always doing. *Doesn't the water feel divine, Jeffrey,* she might have said as she walked toward him, shaking her hips back and forth like an old-time movie actress.

Then she imagined what was happening right now. Lord knows what embarrassing things Morgan was telling him while she hid in the lake.

Suddenly she desperately needed more air. She shot her head above the water and immediately started to cough and heave.

Jeff and Morgan were standing right there watching her.

"Smooth move, ex-lax," Morgan said, as if Ava wasn't horrified enough.

But Jeff was just smiling at her. The sun shining behind his head made his hair glow, as if he'd dropped straight down from heaven.

"Hey do you want to get a lemonade with me?" he asked.

Before she could stop herself, she turned around to make sure he was really asking her, Ava Lewis, to go and get a lemonade with him.

"He means *you*," Morgan hissed.

Ava stared at him, stunned. He'd never spoken to her before. For a moment she thought this might be some kind of practical joke. A few months before a few of the popular kids had gotten together and told poor Beth Miller that Ian Franklin wanted to "go with her." Everyone knew that Beth was madly in love with Ian. Beth said yes right away and went up to Ian, who actually laughed when Beth called him her boyfriend. Beth had cried and gone home early. It was awful.

But this was Jeff Jackson in the flesh and he didn't seem to be joking.

She stared at him so long he started to smile, then break into laughter. "Come on, it's just a lemonade," he said. "I won't kidnap you, I promise."

"Okay," she croaked. Her face burned with embarrassment. She was such a dork.

She glanced back at Morgan as they walked away together, and her friend smiled and gave her the thumbs-up sign. Ava quickly looked away.

Jeff was as smooth and relaxed as ever, striding beside her. They passed a group of the popular girls, who must have all just arrived, and she could feel them eyeing her. Especially Jennifer Halverson, who did not look at all happy. Ava walked with her chin up, trying not to think about them all staring at her—not only walking with Jeff Jackson but in a *bathing suit* no less. She sucked in her stomach.

"I never really talked to Morgan before," Jeff said. "She's pretty funny."

"Yeah," she said. She tried to think of something to add but her mind went pathetically blank. It always went blank when she needed to say something important.

"She says you live alone with your dad, who's some kind of professor?"

"Yeah."

"My dad is, too. That's what I want to be, a professor."

"Of what?" she asked.

"I'm not sure," he said. "Maybe bugs."

"Bugs?"

"Yeah, I love them. I collect beetles."

"Oh."

Fortunately, they walked up to the lemonade stand right then, so Ava didn't have to say anything about his gross collecting habits.

"Two lemonades," Jeff said, pulling out a five-dollar bill.

"Thank you," she said, taking the drink. She took a sip, and it was like drinking candy. She smiled at him happily.

"You want to walk over to the carousel?" he asked.

"Sure," she said, wondering if he was going to start looking for beetles. She thought if he did, she might die.

The music from the ride, old-timey and tinny, was blaring from the old wooden structure. It was one of Ava's favorite places in the world. Even with all the disgusting bug talk, she couldn't imagine anything better than this moment, right now. Summer was here, and she was drinking a lemonade by the carousel with the cutest boy in school.

That is when she noticed a weird kind of itching on her arms. She tried to scratch them nonchalantly as they walked over to the multicolored carousel animals bobbing up and down.

"My favorite is the deer with the antlers and jewel eyes," she said, to distract him.

"Where?"

She turned, shifting her back to him and furiously scratching her arm, and pointed. "That one."

"Oh yeah," he said. "I like that one. But my favorite is the lion." And then he gave her a funny look. "Is something wrong?" he asked.

"Like what?" she asked, dropping her arms and turning back to him with wide eyes. It was a look she'd practiced in the mirror. Wide eyes, like Marilyn Monroe.

"Um, I think you're like bleeding or something. In back."

The carousel spun around and around, flashing its lights. Out of the corner of her eye, she could see Jennifer and her friends approaching.

Bleeding? She felt the oddest sensation then, a prickling across her arms and shoulders, down her back. As if she'd gotten tangled up in brambles in the forest. And then she started to itch all over.

"Are you okay?"

She tried to stammer an answer, but just made a strange strangled sound instead. She wanted to scratch herself *everywhere*. What was happening to her? She thought about Lucy Spiegel, how she'd spent a whole day last year walking around school with her skirt tucked into her underwear. And now here Ava was, standing in front of everyone in her new bathing suit, with some hideous thing happening to her body that she couldn't even see. Her mind spun in horror.

Before it got any worse, she turned and ran. Past the lemonade stand, past Jennifer and her friends, past the beginning of the beach line and over to the bathrooms. Her skin prickling and itching. She touched her arms as she ran, and felt little bumps that hadn't been there before. Thankfully, the girl's room was empty and she rushed inside and slammed the door shut.

Scratching furiously, she peered into the mirror at her own horrified face and then at her arms and shoulders, the strange bumps she'd felt under her fingers. As if . . . something was growing from her skin.

Just then, another feather drifted into the air. Bright white, like the one in her father's workroom.

Was it coming from... her? It seemed her body was always playing tricks on her nowadays. Everything growing, changing, becoming monstrous and gross and strange...

Outside, someone started banging on the door. "Are you okay, Ava?" It was Morgan. "Ava, what's going on? Why'd you run away like that? He's gonna think you're crazy."

She moved right next to the door and pressed her lips to the crack.

"Morgan," she said, whispering as loudly as she could. "Can you bring me my cell and my clothes?"

"What's going on? Ava, you're being crazy!"

"Just bring them! Please!"

"Okay, okay. You know, other people need to get in here."

"Then hurry! Run!!"

All she wanted now was to get out of there. Get back to her pale pink room and shut the door. Then she could cry as much as she wanted to. All she had to do was hold herself together till then.

A few minutes later, Morgan was back, yelling for Ava to open the door.

Ava opened it a crack, grabbed her clothes and phone, and then pushed it shut again. "Just give me a minute," she yelled, slipping back into her clothes and trying to dial her father at the same time.

He answered on the first ring. "What is it?"

"Dad," she said. "Please come get me. Right away."

To her surprise, he didn't ask any questions. "I'll be there in fifteen minutes," he said. "Will you be okay until then?"

"Yes," she said.

"Then wait for me in the parking lot." They hung up, and she looked once more into the mirror, ignoring Morgan and other voices now, just outside the door.

Other than her watery, terrified eyes, she looked normal.

A normal almost-thirteen-year-old who couldn't stop scratching her weird, pale, not-even-slightly-tan skin.

She slipped on her T-shirt and shorts, then opened the door and left the bathroom. An angry woman pushed past her inside.

"What's wrong?" Morgan asked, her face pained. "What happened?"

"Nothing," Ava said. She felt bad for her friend, who was so worried, but what could she say to her? She had no idea what was wrong. All she wanted to do was curl up and die. "I just want to go home."

"Okay." Morgan reached out and hugged her, and Ava hugged her back. "I'll tell Jeff you only freak out like a looneytunes on Sundays."

Ava smiled. Morgan was a good best friend even if she was a huge dork. "I'll text you later."

Her father raced into the parking lot like an ambulance driver, looking visibly relieved to find Ava all in one piece.

"What's going on?" he asked, as she slipped into the car. "Are you hurt?"

"I'm fine!" she said, folding her arms and turning to the window.

"You're fine?"

She held back tears. "Dad, please! I just need to go home!"

He looked at her and sighed. "Ava, don't you find this behavior a little odd? Are you trying to give your old dad a heart attack?"

"You're not that old," she lied, leaning her forehead

against the glass. In the distance, she could see Jeff and his friends. They were probably all talking about what a complete spazz she was. "Dad, can we just go, please?"

"We're going, we're going," he said, pulling back onto the country road that led to the lake.

After an excruciating ride with her nosy father, Ava ran into her room and closed the door, then pulled off her T-shirt and shorts and bathing suit. A cluster of feathers—tiny ones, little baby feathers—fell to the floor, bloody at the tips.

She looked down at it, then turned her back to the mirror and looked over her shoulder.

Her skin looked strange and jagged and bumpy, but soft, too. Kind of magical. She looked more closely and gasped. There were tiny little feathers all across her back, as if she were some kind of winged animal. They were sprouting all over her back now, across her shoulders and down her upper arms. Some were fully formed feathers, some just the tips, pressing out. And all over, she tingled and itched.

And Jeff had seen!

She started rubbing her palms down her arms, trying to find some relief.

It was too much. Ava moved away from the mirror, lay on her side on the bed.

Monique was curled up by the pillow and Ava pulled her to her chest, but the cat wriggled out of her arms just as another feather wafted into the air. Monique leapt up and swatted at it, watching with fascination as it drifted to the floor.

For a few minutes Ava just lay there. Then she reached out and picked up the photo of her mother that she kept on the nightstand. A black-and-white photo of her staring into the camera. Impossibly beautiful, with inky black eyes and long pale hair.

"Mama," Ava whispered, letting go, letting tears roll down her face. "Please. Come back."

CHAPTER TWO

*A*va had not even been three years old when her mother died, and yet she swore she could remember her, even if those memories were like fragments from dreams.

But she kept those bits of memory close to her heart: the smell of her mother's hair, the feel of her mother's skin as she held Ava in her arms, the image of her laughing in the sunlight. In her closet, she kept a box filled with her mother's things: a scarf, a few pieces of jewelry, a bottle of the perfume her mother wore, which Ava occasionally took out and held to her face, breathing in, imagining she could conjure her mother to her right then. And then she had photos. Like the one next to her bed, which her father had taken one day out in the backyard, under the weeping willow. This was how Ava always thought of her. The sunlight streaming down on her light hair so that it seemed almost white, her beautiful laughing face.

Her mother.

Her father never wanted to talk about her. Though it had been more than ten years since her death, he had never even looked at another woman since. You'd think she was still alive, the way he wore his wedding ring and spoke of her, on the rare occasion that he did at all, as if she were right around the corner. Even Ava knew this was not exactly the most healthy behavior. The only person Ava could *really* talk to about her mother—the only other person who had known her mother, that is, who was still around—was her grandmother, and Grandma Kay was old and losing her memory. Ava's mother didn't even have any family of her own, so when she died there was no one left. No one to remember her, or tell stories about her when she was young.

And so Ava's mother was a secret thing, something only for her.

Sometimes, Ava liked it that way—or maybe she didn't like it, but she was at least okay with it—having this secret mother who lived in dreams and photographs. Other times, like now, she would have given anything to have her mother back. A real mother who would hold her and comfort her and explain what was happening and tell her that everything was going to be okay.

Sitting in front of the mirror in her bedroom, with the door locked, Ava stared at herself in disbelief. She couldn't look away, the sight was so horrible.

In the few hours since she'd returned home from the lake, the itching had stopped but the feathers seemed to be *multiplying* . . . growing up and down her arms, over her shoulders. And they were becoming larger, some as long as her pinky finger. She put her hand over her arm, felt them pushing against her palm. They prickled across her back, her shoulders, her arms. Coating her until it was impossible to see the skin underneath.

She picked a feather up off the floor and brought it to her face. It seemed normal enough, for a feather, though it was bright white and seemed to glitter when the light hit it.

She ignored the plinks coming from her computer and the buzzing coming from her cell—no doubt Morgan IM-ing and texting her to see what had happened. She couldn't deal with Morgan right now, couldn't deal at all with the awfulness of what was happening, and the one big truth that it all pointed to . . .

That she was a *freak*. A total, complete freak.

To think of all the times she'd been embarrassed by her pale skin, her too-tall body, her pooching belly. She'd give anything now, to just go back to normal. Suddenly nothing about her normal life seemed so bad at all. So what if she wasn't one of the popular girls? So what if she could barely speak and in fact had a tendency to dive underwater like a huge dork when Jeff Jackson was around?

Now everything was ruined. She would never be able to show her face in public again. All her dreams of growing up and moving to a big city like New York and maybe getting a job writing for a magazine or owning a flower shop or becoming a psychiatrist were shattered. She would obviously never be able to leave her house again, let alone Pennsylvania or the seventh grade. Not only would Jeff Jackson never like her, but no boy ever. Unless he was blind. And lived in a bubble.

Ava refused to leave her room all that afternoon and evening, even when her father knocked on the door and told her that *Pretty in Pink* was on (she loved old John Hughes movies!) and that he was thinking of ordering a pizza for dinner and would even let her pick the toppings.

"I'm not hungry! And I'm so over that movie," she lied, immediately realizing she was starving. "I'm already in bed."

"Can I bring you anything?"

A new life, she thought. "No!"

"Okay. Well, there will be leftovers in the fridge if you feel better later. Get some rest."

"I'm *trying*," she said, making her voice sound raspy

and weak. There was no way she could go back to school tomorrow. Or anywhere again, ever, for that matter. But how was she going to explain that to her dad?

Later, when the television was silent and the house dark and she knew her dad was in bed, she slipped on her favorite hoodie and tiptoed into the kitchen, grabbed a slice of pizza and a yogurt and went back to her room.

She ate the pizza and yogurt, and then she went back to the kitchen and ate the rest of the pizza, until it was gone. What did it matter? At least she could console herself with yummy food since obviously she could never go out in public again. She imagined her days from now on. Locked in the house, empty pizza boxes strewn around her. She'd end up being like that guy she saw on TV who had to be carried out of his house with a crane. Except of course that guy didn't have feathers.

She moaned out loud. Never in her life had she felt this sorry for herself, or this envious of everyone else. Even the most uncool girl in school was cooler than she was right now. Becky Rainer with her unwashed hair and funny walk and braces with bits of food in them, even *Becky* was cooler than she was. She thought of Becky, with her smooth greasy unfeathered skin, and wanted to cry.

Plus, her stomach hurt now.

She took off the hoodie and lay on the bed, careful to lie with the feathers flat—it hurt, she realized, to bend them, and it was a relief to expose them to the air. She stared out the window. There was a bright, big moon, nearly full, shining through the tree branches, surrounded by thousands of stars. Ava shifted her head, moving her pillow down, until she could stare right into the moon, unobstructed. As soon as she did, she felt her body relax and sleep start to come over her.

Her grandmother had told her to look for her mother in the moon and the stars. "On the night of the full moon," her grandmother had said, "you can see her, sometimes sitting on the moon, sometimes spread out over the stars, flying across the night sky."

The moon glowed behind the trees, and the stars all seemed to be spinning.

"Are you there?" Ava whispered.

The leaves rustled in a slight breeze.

She tried to stay awake, but her eyes were so heavy now. Outside, the breeze picked up, and the tree itself started to sway. The stars made shapes in the sky. The Big Dipper and Little Dipper, which her father had pointed out to her, the day he showed her how to find the North Star. She imagined her mother there, among the constellations, imagined she could make out her mother's long hair, her large eyes, in the stars. And just as she drifted off to sleep, she was sure she saw her mother's face looking down at her, smiling.

When Ava woke, the sun was streaming in through the window. She blinked, disoriented, as her room came to life around her. The pale pink walls and the Ava Gardner poster her grandmother had given her the year before, the little rocking chair covered with discarded clothing. She sat up, yawning. What strange dreams she'd had: She'd been flying, she remembered, great big wings stretched out on either side of her body, the stars surrounding her, the sky like black water, thick and warm.

She reached down to scratch her arm, expecting to find bare skin.

Instead, her hand pushed into a pile of feathers, which ruffled at the contact. Ava gasped and snatched her hand away. Gross!

She leapt up and ran to the mirror.

There she was: her flowing dark hair, her pale skin, her long neck…and then her long arms, covered, from the shoulder to the elbow nearly, with white sparkling feathers. There were so many now! She turned; they were covering her back, too, from her neck and down. Tight and close to her body, like a thin layer of vanilla icing.

There was no way Ava was going to school the next morning, but of course her father might have something to say about that. He did seem to think that school was awfully important, being a professor and a parent and all. She wrapped herself in her comforter until it was covering her arms and back and shoulders, and opened the door of her room. Her father was in the kitchen pouring coffee. She shuffled toward him, coughing and trying to look as miserable as possible.

"It lives!" he said, turning and smiling.

"Barely," she said.

"You look like you need this coffee more than I do, sweetheart."

"Gross. What I need is my bed."

"Well, I'm not sure they let you bring beds to school, do they?"

"Dad," she moaned. "I can't go to school when I'm this sick!"

He cocked his head and looked at her, squinting. "Are you sure this doesn't have anything to do with what happened yesterday, at the lake? You seemed awfully upset. Morgan seemed to think it might have had something to do with one Jeffrey Jackson?"

Ava could have killed Morgan then. "No! Dad, I'm really really sick. I was sick yesterday, too, that's why I was upset."

"Not sick enough to finish off that pizza, though?"

"I have a *cold*," she said, coughing for effect. "You can still be hungry with a cold. Hungrier, even!"

He reached over and put his hand against her forehead, frowning. "Well, no fever. No body parts falling off. Maybe we should make an appointment with Dr. Rose."

"I don't need a doctor, Dad, I can just stay in bed all day and drink lots of OJ."

"Who is this Jeffrey fellow anyway?"

Ava felt herself blush from her forehead to her toes. Yet another weird way her body was betraying her. "He's just a boy at school, Dad."

"Hmm. How very interesting." He smiled and raised his eyebrows, his handsome face crinkling, and then pulled her in for a hug. "You stay in bed and you rest. I'll be home by dinnertime. Call me if you need anything at all, okay?"

"Okay," she said, careful to keep her comforter wrapped tight around her.

She watched her father's old truck pulling out of the driveway and into the street. Outside, the sun was bright and shining. It would be an amazing day. When she was sure her father was a safe distance away, Ava threw off the comforter and ran into the backyard.

No matter how miserable her life was, and how freaky she was becoming, it was still a gorgeous day and one that she didn't have to spend in school like the rest of her friends. And the benefit of living in the middle of nowhere? Was that there weren't many people around to see you when you grew feathers all down your arms and across your back. She spread her arms and laughed. Hey, maybe she could fly. That might semi make up for being a freak.

She took a running leap into the air, but nothing at all

Carolyn Turgeon

happened, and she tumbled onto the grass. The feathers stayed tight on her skin. Her arms remained regular arms. Just really really weird regular arms. She sighed.

Flopping over onto her back, she let the sun soothe her. Immediately she felt better. If only every moment could be like this one: the sun warm and lush on her skin, the earth soft underneath her. The vague sound of sprinklers and birds and cars driving by out on the main road.

The air smelled of freshly cut grass. Her dad must have been busy the day before.

She closed her eyes and dreamed. In her fantasy, she was at the lake wearing her bathing suit, and Jeff Jackson was there, smiling at her, taking her hand. They swam, hand in hand, laughing and pushing through the water. She imagined his wet face emerging from the water, him smiling and gazing at her with those blue eyes of his . . .

He was so cute!

That chin with the dimple in it, his super handsome face and blue blue eyes that made her swoon . . . In her fantasies, she'd laugh and tell stories and jokes that sent him howling with laughter. She was easy and normal and not even slightly shy. She was like Jennifer and the other girls who always looked so confident, like nothing at all bothered them, ever. She couldn't imagine any of them dying of embarrassment the way she, Ava, did every day of her life. She had never seen any of their faces turn pink, and then bright red, the way hers did whenever a teacher called on her and made her speak in front of the class and all she wanted to do was curl up and hide. They were all pretty and perfect and had beautiful, radiant mothers who dropped them off at school and showed up at school dances to make sure no one did anything bad, like when Kyle Summerfield sneaked in beer one time and passed out in the bathroom.

She could practically feel his hand in hers. Her first kiss, her first boyfriend.

She thought about him buying her lemonade at the carousel, how he had looked at her, all the fascinating things she could have said to him.

But the fantasy didn't last. A bird cry snapped her out of it, and she remembered: She was not a girl who could have a boyfriend like Jeff Jackson, or any boy, really. She was a freak, with feathers growing down her arms. How could she ever show her face anywhere? How could she ever go back to school, or to the lake? What would she do tomorrow? She would have to spend her whole life locked up in her bedroom!

Above her head, a bird was swooping down. A swan. Its huge white wings spread out on either side.

Ava gasped, sitting up.

It was so beautiful, and its black, glittering eyes were staring right at her.

She sat as still as possible, afraid to breathe.

For a moment the bird seemed to be floating. And then

it let out a long, trumpeting sound, passing over her so close she could have reached up and grabbed it. She cried out and bent down, covering her head, and then, after a moment had passed, she looked up again as the swan disappeared in the distance, its enormous white wings sparkling in the sun.

It felt like she'd witnessed something magical. Like the time she'd come upon a great buck in the woods, its antlers rising up into the sky, and they'd stood there watching each other, only feet away, before the animal turned and bolted. Amazing.

She leaned back again, feeling happy suddenly. She stretched out her arms and realized they were sort of beautiful, the feathers. Weird, yes. But sort of beautiful.

In a weird way.

The whole day spread out in front of her. She could watch *Pretty in Pink* maybe, if her dad had Tivo'd it, which he probably had, to be nice. Watching Molly Ringwald make that cool pink eighties dress always made her feel better about the world. She could lay out some more, but was there really a point now? She could play video games, or give Monique a new hairdo. Monique hadn't really been looking so sharp lately.

What she really wanted to do, she decided, was see her grandma. It had been at least a couple of weeks since she'd seen her, and you never knew with old people. Grandma Kay was always saying she had one foot in the grave, which made Ava imagine her with one foot in a big hole in the ground, her spindly legs stretching out like taffy. Ava loved her grandmother and her little house that always seemed to smell like gingerbread. Even if Grandma Kay was a little nutty sometimes, as Ava's dad put it, she was the one person who could make everything seem normal again.

When Ava stood, finally, there were white feathers all over the grass. From her or from the swan, she couldn't be sure.

"Great." she said out loud. Shouting after the swan like a crazy person. "That's just great! Thank you!"

It was slow going, trying to shower. Feathers kept clogging the drain and she had to scoop them out and throw them into the toilet so the shower wouldn't overflow. Plus the whole feathers-in-the-drain thing might look sort of funny when her dad got home, she thought. Monique didn't make it any easier, perched the whole time on the toilet, eyeing Ava suspiciously and occasionally voicing her discontent.

It felt surprisingly good though, the water moving over her, and she couldn't help but notice how clean and bright the feathers were after. Even cleaner and brighter than they had been before, which was sort of crazy.

She dressed quickly, tearing through her closet to find the hoodie she'd worn all winter and throwing it on. It seemed to cover everything all right as long as she kept the sleeves down and the hood on her head. Which might look strange to anyone else, wearing long sleeves and a hood in the summer sun, but not as strange as it'd look to be covered in feathers. She could just pretend she was delicate and cold all the time, like Grandma Kay was. Though Grandma Kay was, like, a thousand years old.

Luckily, Grandma Kay wouldn't notice anything; that she could be sure of. Grandma Kay had started losing her sight some years before and by now was nearly blind. Grandma Kay might be her only friend from now on, come to think of it. Though maybe, Ava thought, it would be possible for her to meet other blind people who would accept her. Blind people! The thought was heartening.

Ava felt like a spy as she cut through the woods and took back roads to Grandma Kay's. She loved this route: the wildflowers growing along the sides of the roads, the sweet little houses with porches wrapping around them, the big swaying trees. It might have been a nowhere town, but it was awfully pretty. She loved the little park on her grandma's side of town, with the treehouses and the merry-go-round covered with pictures of snails.

Grandma Kay lived in a house that felt more like home than anywhere Ava had ever been. As she approached, she already started feeling like everything would be all right. But how could it be, really?

"Grandma!" she called, pushing through the screen door in back, which was never locked.

There was no answer.

"Grandma!"

"Is that you Ava?"

"Yes, where are you?"

"In here!"

Ava followed her voice into the den, where her grandmother sat in her old chair, rocking back and forth. A small, elegant woman, she was beautifully dressed in a filmy top and skirt.

"What are you doing, Grandma?" Ava asked, concerned.

"Just sitting here, thinking about your grandfather."

"Oh." Ava sat down on the couch. "Don't be sad, Grandma."

"I'm not sad at all honey. How are you, doll? Shouldn't you be at school?"

"I stayed home sick today."

"Is that right? And yet you managed to make your way here. I'm so impressed!"

Ava laughed. "Well." Her grandma always seemed to know when she was lying. She seemed to know lots of things.

"Is everything all right with you, Ava? Your grandfather seems to think that you're having a hard time right now."

Ava hesitated. "But, umm. Grandpa is dead, Grandma."

"I can still talk to him, though, dear."

"Really? How?"

"He lives in here." Grandma Kay pointed to her chest,

where her heart was.

Ava felt tears spring to her eyes. "Oh. Well. I just . . . I don't know what to do. Something is . . . happening to me. Like, with my body."

Her grandmother smiled, fixing her pale blue eyes on Ava. "You're becoming a young woman, dear. Your body does all kinds of things at this age. Don't be afraid of what's happening. It's natural. More natural than you think."

Ava looked at her grandmother. Did she know? She had the oddest expression on her face, as if she were looking at a ghost. It was the same kind of expression she'd had when she read Ava's palm or laid out her tarot cards, when Ava was a kid. Grandma Kay had always been funny like that, and Ava and Morgan had loved to spend afternoons over here when they were little, listening to Grandma Kay talk about love lines and hangmen and magicians. But that was before Grandpa died and Grandma Kay started losing her vision and Ava's father told Grandma Kay to stop with the kooky stuff altogether. "You're corrupting their pure young minds," he'd said.

Ava shook her head.

Of course Grandma Kay didn't know.

She sighed. "It's not natural, though, what's happening. It's . . . weird. And gross." Ava almost took off the hoodie to show her grandmother the feathers, or at least let her feel them, but then she stopped herself. What could her grandmother, a blind old woman, do to help? Grandma Kay might have been kooky (and wonderful!), but she couldn't make miracles happen. Ava just wanted to see her, be here. Lie for a while on the couch and talk to her grandma while eating ginger snaps out of the box.

Forget, and feel like everything would be fine.

"Honey, you're becoming who you're going to be. That I know. And you're going to be wonderful. All you have to do is sit back and let it happen."

"Sure," Ava said. "Just let it happen."

What other choice did she have?

CHAPTER THREE

When Ava tried to stay home from school a second day, her father would have none of it. Especially when she'd acted suspiciously normal the night before as they sat together watching a movie he'd Netflix'ed for her. An old Ava Gardner movie that actually wasn't too bad for being black and white.

"You should really get to know your doppelganger," he'd said.

"Doppelganger?"

"Your twin."

She was certainly regretting watching that movie now

and letting her father see her acting so healthy and un-sick. But it was hard to spend hours on end pretending to be sick in bed when it was so beautiful outside, when she'd just spent a long lovely afternoon with her grandmother, and when her father insisted on making his famous Italian meatballs that he rolled by hand, plus a big salad with artichoke hearts and olives, two of her favorite things, and *then* put on a movie with a gorgeous old movie star he claimed was her twin. The movie star she'd been named after, no less.

There were worse twins to have, she had to admit. As her grandmother would say, that Ava Gardner was one tall drink of water even if she was only five foot five.

Now there was no way she could stay home, though she definitely felt sick. Felt like she was dying, in fact. Didn't that horrible feeling in the pit of her stomach count for something?

"I think it's called I-don't-want-to-go-to-school-itis," her father said. "Believe me, I've had it, too. And why have you suddenly decided to wear a hoodie every day in June? What's going on under there? Do you think Ava Gardner ever wore a hoodie?"

"Dad, I'm twelve!" she cried, and then ran into her room and slammed the door.

How could she possibly go to school and face Jeff Jackson and Jennifer Halverson and all the rest of them? Not only did she have thick white feathers all down her arms and across her shoulders and back, but now the skin around the feathers seemed to be wrinkling, drying up, separating. It was getting worse! And even more gross, which hadn't seemed possible the day before. By this time next week she could look just like Big Bird.

The hoodie hid everything, but on top of looking totally ridiculous in this weather, it also made her look like she'd gained twenty pounds.

Which she hadn't. At least not *yet*.

"Ava, you are going to school if I have to drag you there by that ridiculous hood!" her father yelled, banging on the door. "You have less than two weeks left, all your exams, and no child of mine is going to fail the seventh grade!"

"How can they fail me for being *sick*!" she yelled back, from behind the door.

She knew she was being ridiculous, but what was she supposed to do? It was all so unfair!

"Ava, we both know you are not sick. If you'd tell me what is actually going on, I could possibly help you. You can tell me anything, you know. Whatever's going on with you. I am an adult and fairly intelligent as well."

"You can't help me!" she said, throwing open the door. A dramatic gesture worthy of a movie star, she thought, Ava Gardner flashing through her mind. "You would never understand!"

Her father rolled his eyes and threw up his hands. "You're

not even a teenager yet, Ava. What am I going to do with you? Now get dressed and I'm taking you to school myself."

"Fine," she said, slamming the door shut again and throwing herself onto her bed.

She would just have to wear hoodies every day until school was over and then she had the whole summer to lock herself in her room—well, maybe hang out in the backyard, and in the woods, and in the den in front of the big-screen television, and maybe at Grandma Kay's house, though only if her father dropped her off and she rode in the trunk of the car—to be a freak by herself. And after that? She'd obviously have to run off and join the circus.

That wasn't a bad idea, she realized. Imagining herself, suddenly, covered in white feathers, her black hair piled on top of her head, riding around on the top of an elephant. The crowds would laugh and roar and applaud as she guided the elephant around the ring. Maybe she'd stand on the elephant's back and wave a baton with tassles on the end the whole time. Tassles on *fire*.

"Ava!"

"I'm coming!" she said, jumping up from the bed and throwing on her hoodie and a pair of jeans, a feather drifting to the ground behind her.

She grabbed her school bag and her cell phone, which she flipped open for the first time in two days. She'd finally silenced it the night before to avoid Morgan's calls. Now she had thirty-one missed calls, and nearly twenty text messages. At least Morgan loved her. Morgan *was* like her sister. Maybe Morgan would still love her when she turned into a giant bird.

"WHERE RU?" was the last text.

Ava wrote back. "Was sick, coming today."

She spent the rest of the ride deleting her in-box, one message from Morgan after another, until they pulled up to the front of the ugly gold brick building with the words HOUGHTON MIDDLE SCHOOL across it.

"Are you sure you don't want to talk about it?" Ava's father asked, turning to her. "Or at least take off that hood?"

He looked so loving and worried. She felt terrible for him suddenly. Not only had he lost his wife and never really even looked at another woman since, but now his daughter was covered in feathers and very likely going to join the circus or go live in a cave. On impulse, she reached over and kissed his cheek.

"I'll think about it, Dad," she said. "Thank you for driving me to school and caring so much about my education even though I am deathly ill."

He laughed. "No problem, kiddo. I love you, too. Now go knock 'em dead."

The school loomed up in front of her, kids standing all around and hanging out on the front steps. She took a deep breath. It was worse than she thought. It was as if no one had ever seen a girl in a hoodie on a hot June day before. She walked hunched over, with her head down, but she could still feel everyone staring.

It *was* hot. High of ninety degrees, the weather forecast had said. Already she was starting to sweat, which made her feathers stick together. As if she didn't feel like enough of a freak already. Everyone else was dressed as if they were living in a California beach town rather than the center of Pennsylvania. Louis Woods was even wearing a surfer shirt that hung to his orange fake-tanned legs. Ridiculous.

And right there by the front doors, Jeff Jackson was standing alone. She glanced up and met his eyes. He was staring at her. She could feel herself blushing wildly. He had to think she was completely mad after what had happened, not to mention hideous and deformed and totally impolite. But to her surprise, he smiled and waved.

Immediately she looked down, and then caught herself and looked up again, forcing herself to wave back. Ava Gardner would have waved back. The circus star who could stand on an elephant and twirl batons would have waved back. She forced herself to keep walking, even though every instinct told her to turn around and run. Her heart was pounding in her chest. What if feathers started spilling from her body and onto the ground?

He obviously wanted to talk to her. He was actually

smiling and gesturing for her to come over.

Nervously, she walked toward him. She wracked her mind for something to say, to explain her strange behavior at the lake. Maybe she could explain that her body had been temporarily taken over by extremely dorky aliens? Maybe he found it charming that she lacked any kind of social grace?

As she walked toward him, a group of girls burst out of the front doors of the school and skipped down the stairs. Within seconds Jeff was surrounded.

"Jeff!" they called, giggling. "What's going on?" one voice in particular asked. Jennifer Halverson's voice. Of course.

Jeff gave Ava a small smile and a shrug as Jennifer threw her arms around him.

Awkwardly, Ava changed direction to pass the group of them on the left, and almost stumbled.

"Nice outfit," Brenda Mulligan called out. Brenda was one of the small group of girls who seemed to follow Jennifer everywhere. A zombie, Morgan called her. "All those girls are zombies," Morgan had said. "Except they don't even *want* brains!"

Ava ignored the group's laughter. If they were laughing at her, which they probably were, she didn't want to know.

"Hey, cut it out," Jeff said.

Ava looked up in shock. He was defending her! She couldn't believe it. He was so gallant, like Cary Grant. She wanted to run up right then and there and plant one on him.

She gave him a bright smile as she passed, just to annoy Jennifer even more, and a thousand fantasies filled her head as she raced up the front steps of the school.

She imagined herself and Jeff going down a wedding aisle. Her sitting on her elephant and wearing a big white feathered dress, him in his swimming trunks, his tanned muscles gleaming, his handsome face smiling as he vowed to defend her and love her and act just like Cary Grant but even more awesome until they were old and dead.

As she pushed through the front doors, she was jumping down from the elephant's back and into Jeff Jackson's arms.

"Ava!" Morgan's voice called out, piercing through the hallway chatter.

Ava tried to pretend she couldn't hear her friend. Suddenly the hallways seemed impossibly crowded—and dangerous. All she had to do was get to homeroom and she'd be safe. She shouldn't have even been here. What she should have done, she realized, was walk right past the school and loiter all day at the supermarket down the street, or out in the woods like some juvenile delinquent.

"Ava!"

Morgan was right in front of her. Despite herself, Ava was impressed that her friend could move so quickly. Morgan wasn't the most graceful girl ever, not that Ava could talk.

"I have a test, I need to study."

"Bull. What happened?" Morgan stood with her hands

at her waist, refusing to budge. Her red hair wild around her freckled face.

"I got sick. What do you mean?"

"Something *happened*, at the lake. You weren't sick, you freaked out."

"You misunderstood."

"I did *not*. One minute you were making out with the most popular boy in school, the next minute you were freaking out in the bathrooms."

"We didn't make out."

"Whatever. You would have, if you hadn't freaked out."

"Quit saying that!"

They were standing in front of a classroom, and now kids were pushing by them to get inside. People were starting to stare.

"Ava! Why are you being so weird? And why are you wearing that hood?"

Ava took Morgan's hand and started pulling her down the hallway to the girls' bathroom.

"You better tell me what's going on," Morgan said, "if you're going to make me miss homeroom. I already have three tardies, you know."

"Listen, something really terrible is happening, okay?" Ava said, pulling Morgan into the girls' room.

She'd expected to find a safe haven there, but she realized, too late, that they weren't alone. Jennifer Halverson's BFF

Vivienne Witmer was standing at the mirror smearing gloss over her perfect Angelina-Jolie lips.

"I hope everything is okay," Vivienne said, turning to them with exaggerated concern.

"Thanks," Ava said.

"You must really be having a bad hair day," Vivienne said as she walked past and out the door. "See you!"

"She is so unpleasant," Morgan sniffed. "It's just because Jeff Jackson likes you, you know. Now are you going to tell me what's going on or not?"

Ava studied her friend. If she had to tell anyone, it would be Morgan. She probably should tell someone what was going on in case the feathers killed her or something, or she suddenly turned into a giant bird. But just the thought of talking about it out loud made her feel sick.

"How bad can it possibly be? We live in Pennsylvania and we're *twelve*. Do you have some weird rash or something?"

"No!"

"Why do you have your head covered? Did you get a bad perm? Or cut off all your hair?" Morgan's eyes widened. "Oh my god, you shaved your head."

"Why would I shave my head?"

"You totally liked that girl's shaved head on *America's Next Top Model*. You did it, didn't you?"

"No!"

"Do you need me to help you shop for a wig?"

"No, I do not."

"Ava, look on the bright side. You could get a pink bob or something."

"*Okay*," Ava said. "I'll tell you what happened, and what's happening, but you won't believe it. And you have to swear you will not tell one single other soul."

"I swear!"

"But I can't tell you here. Can you come over after school? My dad gets home around six so we'll have a couple of hours."

Morgan crossed her arms and leaned against one of the sinks. "You can't make me wait until after school. It's only first period! Which we are missing, by the way, thankyouverymuch."

"You might freak out when I tell you."

"I promise not to freak out, okay? No matter what it is."

"You swear?"

"Yes!"

Ava took another deep breath. Outside, the halls were quiet now. Normally she would never have skipped a class, but nothing about today was normal, was it? She thought wistfully of her straight A's and how little good they would do her in the world now. Obviously, it was all downhill from here.

Morgan stood waiting, her big green eyes watching Ava worriedly, impatiently.

"Let's go into a stall," Ava said. "Just in case anyone comes in. And then I'll show you. The one at the end."

"Okay," Morgan said.

Ava checked all the other stalls, just to be sure, even though all the doors were wide open. She would die if anyone overheard what she was about to tell her friend.

And then she followed Morgan into the last stall and latched the door.

"Okay," Ava said. "So ..."

Her voice caught in her throat. To her surprise, she started to cry.

"Ava," Morgan said softly, reaching out to touch Ava's arm, "whatever it is I will help you. You're my best friend."

Ava nodded. Even with Morgan, it was so unbelievably embarrassing. She had to just do it quickly if she was going to do it at all.

"Well," she said, sighing, "just look, then. And no screaming."

And she unzipped her hoodie and pulled it off. Under, she was wearing a black Rolling Stones T-shirt her dad had given her, which she took off, too, until she was standing in her flowered bra.

Wincing, she looked up to see Morgan's reaction.

Her friend stood there with her mouth hanging open, staring in wonder.

"You have. . . " Morgan reached out her fingers and

touched Ava's arm.

"Yes. They just started coming in at the lake, and now . . . Well, this."

"Wow. They're . . . "

"Feathers," Ava whispered.

"Beautiful."

Ava just stared at Morgan, who was softly touching the feathers on her arm with a dazzled look on her face. "What?"

"They're beautiful," Morgan said. "It's like you're wearing this completely glamorous, fantastic old feather jacket. It's so amazing. Like in one of those old movies your dad is always making us watch. With all those ladies who lie in bed and faint and stuff."

"But it's *not* a jacket."

"Let me see the back. It totally looks like you're wearing a jacket. Look how they go down your back and stop at your neck, and end perfectly at your elbows. It's totally weird."

"Yeah, thanks, I KNOW it's weird."

"But weird and *beautiful*, Ava. They're all glittery and perfect. Like, if you sold this in a store it would cost a million dollars."

Ava stamped her sneakered foot in frustration. "I can't take it off though! What am I supposed to do??"

Morgan shrugged, and then her face changed. "Wait a second . . . " She furrowed her brows.

"What?"

"Look." Morgan was touching Ava's arm near the elbow, lifting one of the feathers. "It looks like… Like they're starting to peel or something."

"What??!" Ava snatched her arm away in panic. How much worse could it get? The tears returned then, hot and streaming down her face. What was wrong with her? "I'm such a freak!" she cried.

"No, look," Morgan said. "See? When you lift up the feather, it looks like it's starting to peel. And underneath, your skin is perfect. Can you feel that? Like you're . . . shedding or something."

"Oh my god. What is happening to me?"

Morgan was about to respond—though of course she didn't know any better than Ava did what was wrong—when the bell rang outside, signaling the end of first period. Any minute the bathroom would be full of girls.

Quickly, Ava grabbed her T-shirt and slipped it back on. As she was reaching for her hoodie, she noticed the little clump of feathers scattered on the toilet seat and the floor. "Morgan!" She pointed at the feathers, and her friend bent down to pick them up, accidentally knocking into Ava's arm as she did.

Zipping up her hoodie, Ava burst out of the stall just as Jennifer Halverson entered the bathroom with a few of the zombie girls just behind. After flushing the feathers away, Morgan followed Ava out of the stall.

Jennifer laughed. "Having some alone time, girls?" she asked. The zombies all laughed with her.

"Hey, have you seen Jeff around?" Morgan asked, her voice obnoxiously sweet. "He keeps asking about Ava. I think he has a crush or something. Guess we'll go see what he wants!"

And with that, Morgan brushed past the group of them and out the door.

Jennifer stood looking after her, with her mouth open and her hands on her hips. "Did you hear what she just said to me?"

Ava slinked out the bathroom door and into the crowded hallway, avoiding Jennifer's evil glare, adjusting her clothes so that no feathers would show, peeling or not.

CHAPTER FOUR

*T*he rest of the day passed by in a haze of embarrassment and humiliation—which wouldn't have been so different from most other days for Ava, except that this time there was actually a reason for it. School seemed to last forever, even worse than usual. In gym class, she had to muster every ounce of emotion to convince the teacher she was too sick to participate, and then she had to spend the whole class sitting in the grass next to Alison Freeman, watching the other girls play soccer as sweat rolled down her back, in and out of the feathers, and Alison went on and on about some Broadway musical she'd just seen as well as her great love for field hockey.

It was, truly, the worst hour of Ava's life.

Morgan was no help at all, rushing to find her between classes and staring at her with big googly eyes, offering Ava her arm as if she were an old lady.

"I may have feathers all over me," Ava was forced to say under her breath at one point, "but I can still *walk*, Morgan."

Morgan had just opened her eyes even wider and whispered back, "I bet you can fly, too. Do you want me to help you find out?"

"No!"

By the time Ava got home, she thought she might pass out from heatstroke, not to mention humiliation and mortification generally. The house was empty, except for Monique spread out lazily on the couch in front of the television, licking her paws and staring at Ava suspiciously.

"What?" Ava asked, putting her hands on her hips.

Monique narrowed her eyes and placed her paw on one of the fake fur pillows Ava had insisted her father buy. "Ava Gardner would totally have pillows like this," she'd argued at the time.

"Whatever," Ava sighed, heading to her room and tossing her backpack onto the floor. Behind her, Monique let out a loud yowl.

Ava pulled off the horrible hoodie and collapsed on her bed. She clicked on the ceiling fan and let the air move over her. The feathers were so thick now. Why couldn't she have grown feathers in the wintertime? They might have come in handy then. She closed her eyes and tried to pretend she was somewhere far away. The air and coolness felt wonderful, amazing against her skin, ruffling through the feathers.

She turned over onto her stomach and stretched out. It felt so good, the cool air. She relaxed into the bed, let her mind drift . . .

She woke up disoriented, wrapped in covers. The room was dark. Monique was spread out beside her and moonlight spilled into the room through the window. So bright and silver and glittering, bathing her.

The windows were open, and cool air was blowing down on her from the fan whirring above her on the ceiling. She pulled in the covers more tightly around her.

For a few minutes, she barely knew where she was.

She looked around for a clock. 10:05, it said. It took her a moment to realize: 10:05 p.m. At night. She must have slept all through the evening. Slowly, the day came back to her, a sick feeling in her gut as she remembered school, the way everyone had stared at her, how uncomfortable she'd been.

And Jeff Jackson, defending her. Her heart fluttered. It hadn't been *that* bad a day, when it came down to it.

She got up, throwing off the covers, and pulled on her hoodie again. She tiptoed out of her room. She was hungry, she realized. Starving, in fact.

Her father's bedroom door was open and his bed still made. No wonder the house was so quiet; even if her father were home and asleep, she'd at least hear a snore or two. There was a note on top of the television: "Out fishing, back late. Dinner's in the fridge."

She froze. Realized, all of a sudden, that she'd fallen asleep with the bedroom door open . . . He had to have seen her, checked in on her at least. She felt a sudden resentment that he hadn't awakened her for dinner. And now she was starving and had to fend for herself! But more importantly, she thought, catching herself: Wouldn't he have seen? When had she pulled the covers around herself? Her heart pounded. Plus she hadn't been wearing a shirt! So she was weird, gross, and perverted, all at once. She felt guilty, as if she'd done something horribly wrong and been found out.

The thought crept up on her: but she hadn't done anything, had she? Maybe if he saw, and knew, he could help her.

Immediately she dismissed the idea. Her father had already dealt with the death of his wife, and plus now his own mother not only had one foot in the grave but was also talking to her dead father as if it was perfectly natural. She, Ava, was all he had.

How could she tell him she was covered in feathers?!

She sighed and wandered to the kitchen. As she crossed the living room, she caught sight of the full moon over the mountains in the distance, through the big sliding glass door.

Of course. Her father always went fly fishing on nights of the full moon. He had for as long as she could remember, though Grandma Kay had told her once that he'd become much more regular and even fanatical about it after his wife died, as a way to cope. *That is what the moon is for*, she'd said. *It lets him see her again.*

Grandma Kay always talked that way, though.

Ava stared at the moon now. Perfectly round in the sky, a bright, glowing coin. Its light turned the whole house to silver. Outside, the trees swayed, and a wind rattled the leaves. It was spooky, but beautiful, strange, like something out of a dream. Everything seemed so otherworldly at night. Especially with the full moon outside and her father out fishing.

Her dad always said that fishing by moonlight was the best, that the trout were different somehow, surfacing for the bright light and getting confused and dazzled when it was not the sun that greeted them. He'd stay out all night and fish until dawn, but he was always happy the next day, glowing even. "They swim right to you," he said. "You could scoop them up with your hands." The forest, too, turned magical under the moon, he said, revealing all its secrets.

"Whatever floats your boat," was her typical response. More trout to throw right back in the water. She always thought how terrible it would be to be a fish in these parts, getting caught over and over again whenever you just wanted to swim to the surface and get some dinner.

Speaking of which ... Her growling stomach broke the mood, and she padded over to the kitchen to see what goodies her father had left behind.

Inside, right in the middle of the top shelf, was a Tupperware bowl with a note that said "DINNER, HEAT THREE MINUTES, FROM DAD" taped to the top. She peeked, saw it was his famous spaghetti bolognese, one of her favorites.

Things were starting to look up.

She poured herself a glass of lemonade and stuck the food in the microwave, then wandered back over to the sliding door as the rich scent of meat and sauce began to fill the house.

A figure moved and she cried out loud, almost dropping her drink, before she realized it was her own reflection she was looking at. She stopped, staring at herself. She looked ...pretty. Even in her stupid hoodie. Tall and lean, her long black hair curling down and her skin pale, ivory, which was nice in this light. Beautiful, even. She set down her drink and stepped forward, curious.

She was entirely alone. Her father wouldn't be home for hours yet.

She unzipped the hoodie and pulled it off. Watched as the feathers spread from underneath her short sleeves down to her elbow, catching the moonlight and seeming to glitter.

She stepped forward again, focusing in on her reflection in the glass. Shadows fell over her body, but the feathers glimmered and shone in the light, bright as the moon. Her hair fell black down over them. The feathers did really look like a jacket of some kind, like Morgan had said. She twisted around and looked over her shoulder, lifting up her hair to see the feathers covering her back, spreading up to her neck and down to her hips, but perfectly. As if someone had painted in an outline for them to fill.

She turned back around, moving her hair to cover her breasts.

It wouldn't be so bad, she thought, if she could always just walk about at night in the shadows, seeing her reflection in dark glass, by the light of the moon. She could hang out with vampires and wear lots of black.

Turning again, she put her palm on her forearm and moved it up, slowly, over her skin and to the feathers.

To her surprise, she could slip her hand in between the feathers and her skin. Right there, near her elbows, the feathers were no longer attached. She almost cried out, it was so unexpected, though Morgan had said something about it earlier in the day. Hadn't she? *Peeling*, she had said. *It looks like it's starting to peel . . .*

Ava had blocked it out until now. It had been hard enough just to get from class to class, insisting she was fine even as sweat dripped all over her and she was about to die of heatstroke or humiliation, whichever came first.

She pushed her fingers up farther and felt more feathers coming off her skin, as if she actually *were* wearing a jacket, or, worse, picking a scab. The feathers were all stuck together now, it seemed, as if they'd grown into each other. She winced as she felt them come off her skin, as she lifted the feathers and pulled.

It was so gross. There was a slight sucking sound as the feathers pulled off. She reached up to feel her skin underneath, and her fingers stuck into what felt like a web.

She stopped, shuddering, and sat down on the couch, away from the sliding doors now. Catching her breath, she tried not to throw up. Pulling off the feathers couldn't be more gross than actually having them, could it?

She took a deep breath, and pulled some more, terrified she would rip off her own skin or do something similarly awful.

She whimpered out loud. Monique gave her a disgusted look from across the room.

"*You* try growing feathers and then peeling them off," Ava grumbled. Monique rolled her eyes and slinked away.

There was a sound from outside. Quickly, Ava grabbed her hoodie and slipped it on. Feathers fell to the floor.

Had someone seen?

She shuffled to the sliding door and then peeked through,

pressing her face against the glass.

It took her a minute to focus past her own reflection, through the glass and to the yard outside.

There, right in the middle of the grass, was a bright white swan. Ava blinked. She must be dreaming, she thought. This was all so *weird*. When did swans start hanging out in the backyard? She could swear the swan was watching her, too.

Ava took a deep breath, yanked the door open, and stepped outside.

The swan didn't move.

It just stood there . . . staring at her.

It was really beautiful, glittering and shimmering in the moonlight. Ava thought about other swans she'd seen, randomly in her life, like when she and her dad visited her uncle in this city in Florida that had a big lake filled with swans as well as swan sculptures scattered all through town. Her favorite had been a huge bejeweled one painted pink and purple.

But those swans had been sort of . . . ungainly. Strutting around and honking and stretching their long beaks around and burying them in their own feathers.

This one wasn't ungainly at all. It stood there quietly, soft, like a cat.

"Hello?" Ava whispered.

Beyond the swan and the grass the trees rose up and the woods began. A faint breeze passed over the yard and in the distance, the leaves rattled.

Ava stepped forward.

"Are you watching me?"

She almost expected the swan to answer, and was a little surprised when it just stood there, unmoving, staring at her. A second later, in a swift movement that scared her, made her gasp, it lifted its wings and swooped into the air, disappearing into the woods.

Ava sighed. Not even swans wanted to be hanging out with her now!

And then it hit her.

Of course.

It seemed crazy that it hadn't occurred to her before.

She was growing feathers, there were all these swans popping up everywhere, with their shimmering, glittering feathers, just like her own . . .

Was she turning into a *swan*? Her mind raced. Had she been bitten by a swan . . . in her sleep or something?

Like . . . SPIDER MAN?

Hadn't he been bitten by a RADIOACTIVE SPIDER or something?

The world seemed to spin around her.

Had she been bitten by a radioactive swan???? What did a radioactive swan look like? Did they glitter? Did regular swans who *weren't* radioactive glitter in moonlight?

She entered the house in a daze and flopped down onto

the couch, her mind swirling.

She tried to think of when she might have been bitten by a radioactive swan. She must have been sleeping. Wouldn't she remember something like that? But then she imagined herself saving kittens trapped in trees with her incredible swan powers. Stopping crimes and arresting bad guys. She'd probably have to move someplace where there *were* bad guys. Her dad would have to let her if she was a superhero, right? She wondered if Jeff Jackson would be impressed when he found out, or if it would be too intimidating for him. Maybe he had a secret superhero identity as well? If not, perhaps she could find a radioactive swan to bite him, too.

Then she bolted up in horror.

What if he wanted to be bitten by a radioactive beetle?

Ava tried to calmed herself. The feathers were obviously making her crazy. Totally, one thousand percent looneytunes.

She stood up and took a deep breath, then went to her bedroom and turned on the light. Superheroes were nice and all, but she wanted to be normal. Just a normal girl.

She could save kittens as a normal girl, too. Maybe she would ask her dad if they could go to the SPCA tomorrow. Monique was probably lonely; it's what probably put her in such a bad mood all the time.

And so she closed her eyes, grabbed hold of the feathers on her left arm, at the base, just above her elbow, and pulled.

The feathers came off with a surprising ease now, almost

as if they were pushing themselves into her hands. Even though it was an unpleasant feeling, she did not allow herself to stop.

The feathers pulled off, making a soft, gross *squiching* sound, and leaving a paper-like, web-like film over her skin.

It was gross and beautiful and astonishing and horrifying all at the same time.

She kept pulling. Finally, the whole thing came off. In one piece, all the feathers. She sat in shock for a moment, holding the feathers in her hand, letting the garment—that's what it was, some kind of jacket—stretch out, the end falling down and scraping the floor. It seemed to have a life of its own. A strange energy, filling the room.

She dropped it onto the floor in horror, watched it smooth out as if it were letting out its breath, and stumbled to the bathroom.

Flicking on the light, she expected a hideous sight to greet her. Her skin disgusting and covered in webs, dead skin, god knows what else. By now she'd believe anything at all.

She blinked against the fluorescent light. And blinked again.

Her skin was perfect. She turned around and looked at her back, over her shoulder, but it was fine. Better than fine. It was her old self staring back at her, and yet . . . her skin was creamy and smooth now, like milk, or porcelain. Her hair looked shiny and thick, falling down, covering her slight breasts. And there was something else, something less easily definable. She seemed older, more poised or something. More, she realized then, like her mother. A kind of carriage her mother had had that was clear in every photo of her.

Had she imagined the feathers? Suddenly everything seemed so unreal. Ava ran back to the living room, and the feathers were still there, on the floor. She bent down and ran her palm across them, and they were soft, wonderful. As soft as the fancy mink coat hanging in her grandmother's closet, from the olden days, way back when.

She lifted the garment and hugged it to her. It smelled clean and fresh, like winter. The feathers tickled her nose. It was like a giant pet, wasn't it? A much sweeter, softer one than Monique.

Suddenly, a knock came from the front door. Ava froze on the living room floor, horrified. It was just after midnight; her father wouldn't be home for hours.

Immediately, she shoved the feathered garment under the couch, as if it were a suitcase full of stolen diamonds. She pulled on her hoodie, a habit by now, and tiptoed to the front door. Trying to walk so softly that no one could hear, so that she could pretend that no one was home. Monique padded along with her, rubbing herself against Ava's ankles.

Barely breathing now, Ava stood on her toes and looked through the peephole.

It took a second for her eyes to adjust, focus in.

Outside was a woman with long, glowing white hair. She was dressed in a pale dress, and awash in moonlight. Her eyes were icy blue, enormous jewels. And she was staring directly at Ava.

Ava jumped back, terrified. She had to remind herself that the woman could not see her. Then she looked back through the keyhole.

The woman knocked again. She was so beautiful. Why would a woman like that be knocking on their door?

Ava opened the door, her hands trembling.

The woman smiled at her, and it was the kind of smile that felt like cookies in the oven, warm and comforting. Ava smiled back despite herself, even though her heart was pounding and she was more scared than she had ever been. She could feel Monique cowering at her feet.

"Ava," the woman said, and her voice was soft and musical. "My name is Helen. I've come to see you." She spoke as if it were perfectly normal to arrive at someone's doorstep for the first time, past midnight, and on a school night no less, being totally beautiful and glowing and having eyes like jewels.

The image of the swan flashed across Ava's mind. She shook her head, disoriented.

"How do you know my name? Who are you?"

"Well," the woman said. "I know your mother. I have a message from her."

"My mother?"

"Yes. I was sent here by your mother. There are things you need to know."

CHAPTER FIVE

he whole world seemed to have been remade in silver. The Brooks' house across the street, the trees outside, the pathway leading from the front door to the street, her father's old truck sitting in the driveway. This moon-haired woman at the door.

Ava stared at the woman, confused. "My mother is dead," she said. "She died when I was a baby."

The woman looked surprised, slightly, for a moment, and then said, gently, "Dear, she is dead . . . to this world. But there is more that you don't know yet."

Ava stepped back. "Are you a ghost? Have you come

to take me to heaven?" She thought of the ghost stories Grandma Kay told her, where spirits appeared to take people to early deaths, though the ghosts in those stories were never exactly movie-star beautiful like this. "I'm too young!"

"I'm not a ghost. But I will explain everything."

Ava narrowed her eyes. "Let me touch your arm to make sure."

Helen held out her arm, and Ava reached out and placed her palm on it, feeling the soft fabric of her dress, and the flesh underneath. *Definitely not a ghost*, she thought, slightly disappointed that her hand hadn't gone straight through. But then who was she?

"If you're not a ghost, then how do you know my mother?"

"I will show you everything if you come with me. You were not old enough, before now, to know the things I'm here to tell you."

"How do I know you're not a robber or a murderer?" Ava had watched *Law and Order* with her dad and knew that you couldn't trust just any stranger who came to your door at midnight.

"Because I know your mother. I know what's happening to you. I know that you're growing a feathered robe and probably have no idea why."

Ava's mouth dropped. "Were you spying on me?" Her mind flashed again to the swan in the backyard.

Helen stepped forward, reaching for Ava's hand. "Ava, we've all been keeping watch over you since you were born. Your mother, too, after she came back to us. You're a very rare, very special girl, you know."

Ava pondered this. She *was* exceptionally bright, she knew. And she was very, very good in math. Her teacher had even called her a shining star once, when she'd solved a complicated multiplication problem more quickly than anyone else in class and won a trophy for it. Of course it was just a picture of a trophy that had been laminated, but still.

Plus, she *had* just grown and shed a feather garment. And she was a doppelganger.

Helen wrapped her hand around Ava's. A jolt went through Ava, and an array of images flashed before her eyes: her mother's inky eyes in the photograph by Ava's bed, the swan in the backyard, its wings spreading in the air.

"So you're saying my mother . . . is alive?"

"Yes," Helen said.

Ava looked at Helen more closely. "If my mother is alive," she said, "why didn't she come herself? And why did she go away in the first place?"

"She had to leave. She never should have been here at all, but she loved your father and so she stayed much, much longer than she should have. And she cannot come here now, Ava. You will understand why, in time."

"Will you take me to her?"

Helen hesitated. Behind her, the leaves ruffled in the breeze. "I can't, yet. But I know what is happening to you. I'm here to help you. If you come with me, I can explain everything."

Ava studied her. What if it was true? The thought was so huge Ava couldn't even really grasp it. The idea that her mother could be alive? Was it possible she really was?

Something told her she needed to go with the woman, even though the woman was a stranger and everything about this seemed strange and wrong and dangerous. Except of course for the woman's kind face, her lovely, melting eyes, her soft voice. But Ava had read the old myths and knew that underneath all that beauty the woman could well be an evil old witch or devil.

"Where do you want to take me?" she asked, narrowing her eyes again.

"Into the woods, where the others are waiting." Helen released Ava's hand and stepped back.

"You're not kidnapping me, right? You can't kidnap me. I have a test tomorrow and if I don't pass it I will totally fail the seventh grade. And there's this boy I like..."

Helen laughed. "No. You will be back here before you know it. I promise."

Ava waited a second, so as not to give in too easily—but of course she would go, how could she not?—and then nodded. "Okay, fine, I'll come. Just give me a minute."

Leaving Helen at the front door, she ran back to her room and grabbed her keys and her cell phone, just in case. Her phone was flashing with messages, no doubt from Morgan, who was probably imagining Ava flying her around like Superman. Ava shoved the phone and keys into her jeans pocket. Monique was at her heels, yowling at her.

"Shoo!" Ava said.

Monique swiped at her feet.

"You're not coming!"

Helen was waiting, and Ava breathed out in relief that she was still there. Despite herself, her heart was all clenched up, and she'd been terrified the woman would disappear as quickly and mysteriously as she'd come. Her mother! Maybe she would really finally have a mother, after all this time. It seemed impossible, but then, she was probably dreaming all this anyway, and even a dream mother was better than no mother at all. She shut the door on Monique's glowering face.

"I'm ready," Ava said.

"Let's go."

They walked around the house and cut through the backyard to the woods. It was as if Helen had taken this path many times before, but Ava was certain she would have noticed a woman like her if she'd ever been in the vicinity. Helen was even more beautiful up close and had that same gentle, delicate quality her mother had had. Ava resisted the urge to reach out and take her hand as they walked.

Helen led Ava into the woods. Their feet crunched under them. Ava glanced back at their little house with the moon shining down on it. She hoped her father wouldn't get back before she did. He didn't need to worry about her any more than he did already.

"I used to live with your mother, Ava," Helen said, glancing back. "My sisters and I. I remember when she met your father."

"You did?" Ava had never heard anything about her mother's life before she had met her father. It was as if her mother had only begun to exist when she'd met him. Hearing this, now, was amazing. "What . . . What was she like? Where was that?"

"A place I'll take you to one day. We lived there with many of our friends. Your mother and I used to love to visit the creek here together, in these woods, and go swimming."

"The creek here? Where my dad goes fishing?"

"Yes." Helen smiled.

Ava had to walk quickly to keep up with her. Helen seemed to walk unnaturally fast, without putting forth any real effort. And she seemed to have no problem navigating the woods in the places where the twisting branches overhead blocked out the moonlight. If it weren't for Helen's graceful white shape next to her, Ava surely would have been lost. In some spots she could barely see in front of her.

"We would go with another of our friends," Helen continued. "The three of us were inseparable. We loved it, swimming together."

"Is that how my mom and dad met, at the creek?"

"Yes," Helen said.

Ava wracked her brain but could not remember her father ever saying anything about this. Nothing about how they'd met, at all. All her own little imaginings started shifting in her brain, and now she pictured the woman from the photos—her mother—swimming in the creek with her friends. A sunny day, in summer, the sunlight dappling the water through the leaves and branches. Her father fishing maybe, maybe swimming himself. He'd grown up here, around the creek. His father had fished the creek, too, and his father before him.

"Your father loved your mother right away. We could see that he did."

"Did she love him right away, too?"

Helen paused. For a moment there was just the soft rustling of the woods, the padding of their feet on the earth, the snapping of twigs they stepped over. "I think she did. It was hard to tell with her sometimes. The thing was, though, Ava, they were never supposed to be together."

"They weren't?"

"Oh no. It was forbidden. Where we come from ... well,

we are not supposed to be with human men. Men like your father."

"What do you mean, human men?"

And just then, they stepped into a clearing. One second the world was dark and hushed, the next the moon was bright overhead, its light pouring down on them.

"Oh!" Ava gasped. "I've never been here before."

"We've wandered a bit from the main path," Helen said, turning to her. She was smiling, her face radiant and her jewel eyes sparkling. Just the way Ava imagined her mother would look.

The air was warm, with a slight breeze pushing through, and everything smelled of grass and earth. Ava stepped into the clearing. In the moonlight, the grass was like a secret pool of water, shimmering and moving. Ava half expected to slip under.

"Is this where you're taking me?" Ava asked, seeing that Helen herself had stopped and seemed to be waiting for something.

"Yes," Helen said, reaching out and grabbing Ava's hand, as if she'd read her mind earlier.

Helen's skin was smooth and cool. Ava clasped her hand back.

She thought, then, about her father, sitting along the side of the creek right now. How close was he? Ava had lost all sense of direction. But she stared up at the moon and imagined him out in this same strange darkness, hearing the same hush of the forest at night, waiting for the dazzled fish to surface from the creek, staring up at the same moon and looking for her mother the way she was right now, the way she always did when the moon appeared bright and full over the earth. Ava thought, for the first time, that it might be nice to join her father sometime, even if it made absolutely no sense to catch the same fish over and over and throw them back in.

Suddenly a bird swooped in from overhead and landed in the clearing.

A swan.

Ava pointed, almost crying out. "That swan!" she said, turning to Helen, whom, to Ava's surprise, didn't seem at all taken aback. "I think I saw it before."

And then another swan swooped down, and another and another, and Ava realized they all looked the same. They kept arriving from the air, and then they emerged from the forest, too, like white shadows, until the clearing was filled with them, appearing from every direction, from the woods and the air.

Ava's heart hammered in her chest. Part of her wanted to run; the other part wanted to stay and see everything, no matter what happened.

She didn't understand how Helen could be so calm. Helen just stood watching them, as if she'd been expecting this to happen, as if she saw something this miraculous happen every day.

The swans were strangely still, the mass of their white feathers gleaming like ice, like freshly fallen snow, over the clearing.

"They have all come," Helen said finally, "to meet you."

"What do you mean?" Ava asked.

"Watch."

And just as she said the word, something happened. The birds . . . transformed. In a movement so quick and surprising Ava could barely register it, the birds had arms and hands and their feathers became feathered robes and suddenly the clearing was filled with beautiful women, each of them holding a feathered robe in her hand.

Ava gasped.

"I have . . . " She pointed, unable to finish her thought.

They were all holding feathered robes, like the one Ava had, shoved under the bed.

And they were naked, their hair streaming down and covering their breasts, their legs pressed together. All pale and blond in the moonlight. Beautiful, smiling, watching her with jewel eyes.

Ava could feel her eyes filling with tears. Was one of them her mother? She had never, in her life, seen anything more astonishing or beautiful than this. And she felt herself fill with light. It was the only way to explain it: the happiness that comes from feeling, even if you don't know why or how, that you've come home. But she was far from home, wasn't she? She had never seen this clearing before and yet she knew these woods, knew every bit of them.

She turned, once again, to Helen.

"We are swan maidens," Helen said, before Ava could ask. "We change in the full moon."

"Swan maidens," Ava repeated. It seemed to her, all of a sudden, the most wonderful thing to be.

"When your mother met your father, it was during a full moon. We were swimming. We loved to swim in the creek in our human forms."

"She was . . . she is a swan maiden?"

"Yes, she is one of us," Helen answered. "She stayed here for a time, but then she had to return to us. She was never meant to live in your world. But she not only lived in your world, she had a child in it. And so you, Ava, you are like us."

"Is that why . . ."

"Yes," Helen whispered, and there were tears sparkling in her eyes, too.

"I have a robe."

"Yes, a feathered robe. Yours will let you transform, too. Put it on, and you will become a swan. Take it off, and you are human again."

Ava felt herself staggering under this new information. Her head couldn't even really contain it. Could it be true?

Anything could be true right now, here, in this moonlit clearing, after what she'd just seen.

One of the maidens stepped forward and approached Ava. "Welcome," she said, in a strange, singsong voice. "We have been waiting for this day. I am Lara."

"Thank you," Ava said. "I'm Ava."

"We know."

It hit her then, what they were saying. That she, Ava Lewis, was a part of this. This magical, wonderful world around her, where swans turned into women, under the full moon. She felt she would burst with the fullness of it. Even if it was a dream, it was the best dream she'd ever had, one she hoped she'd have again and again.

She laughed, then, with delight.

"I wish I had my robe here with me now!" She eyed Lara's robe, and Lara laughed, too.

"We can only transform using our own robes," Lara said. "You should have had her bring hers, Helen."

"I did not want to terrify the girl," Helen said. And then, to Ava: "Lara was with me and your mother that day, long ago."

"Is my mother here, too? Can I see her?"

Helen and Lara exchanged a look. "No," Helen said. "In time you will see her again. But she wanted us to come to you, to explain to you what has been happening to your body. We haven't . . . well it has happened only very rarely, a swan maiden mating with a human, and so we were not certain, but it has been told to us that you would experience a change around your thirteenth birthday. And so we have been watching you. She, too, has watched you."

"My mother?"

"Yes."

Ava thought of the moon, the woman sitting in it. *On the night of the full moon*, her grandmother had said, *you can see her, sometimes.*

"We knew how frightening it would be for you," Lara said. "Your mother has been sick with worry, thinking of you. I hope you feel safe now, though. We are your family. All of us."

Ava looked out at the lot of them. All the beautiful maidens, many of them facing the moon now, their faces tilted up, pressing their feet into the earth, lifting up their arms to the breeze.

Helen lifted her own silvery arms into the breeze. "It is a treat for us," she said. "Being in this form. But you, my dear, you have much more human in you than we do. And yet you are still swan. We don't know exactly what to expect from you, but you will be capable of great things."

"When you return home," Lara said. "Use the robe. Transform. Feel what it is to be the other part of you. The world will become entirely different, when you are in your other form. But that is the world, too, and that is you. Part of who you are."

"So I just . . . put the robe on? It just came off of me tonight." She shuddered, thinking of it. "It pulled off of me."

"You shed it. Like a caterpillar growing a cocoon and then sloughing it off. You're lucky. There's a story of a girl many hundreds of years ago who spent years growing her robe and was only able to transform as an old woman. The moment she put her robe on and transformed, she was so happy, felt so complete, she died right then and there."

"So they won't grow back on me? Now that they have come off? I will be normal now?"

"Yes," Helen whispered. "You will seem normal, anyway, but you have a great power. You can be one of them, and you can be one of us, too. Very few have the freedom to straddle two worlds. One day you will choose, but that is not for a long time yet."

The moon, the forest, the women in the clearing, some of them swans again now, Helen and her jewel eyes and talk about other worlds—it was all too much. Ava stood transfixed, dazzled like the fish in the creek. No wonder her father was able to catch them, again and again. The word came to her: *moonstruck.* Like that movie with Cher. She and those poor trout were all moonstruck.

Helen tilted her head and smiled. "I will take you home now, dear girl. You have a lot to absorb from tonight."

Ava nodded. She was so sleepy, suddenly. She tried to keep her eyes open, to take it all in, in case she was dreaming.

"But when will I see you again?" she asked, her voice slurring a little now, she was so tired.

"The next full moon," Helen answered.

And then, before her eyes, Helen slipped on a robe—one of the others had been holding it—and as she did, her whole body bent down, turned into an *S*, and then she was on the ground, her great white wings stretched out on other side, her glittering blue eyes staring up at Ava.

Lara smiled, gesturing. "Go ahead, sit on her back."

Ava looked at her, and then at Helen. "It won't . . . hurt her?"

Lara laughed. "No. Go ahead."

Ava walked over, tentatively, and stretched one leg over the swan's back. And then she sat down, pressing her legs on either side of the bird's thick, soft body. Lara smiled and slipped on her own robe, and then she, too, transformed, her body slipping down, her neck stretching out, feathers sprouting all over until she was white as glittering snow.

Ava blinked, smiling at the clearing filled with swans that now, one by one, began launching themselves into the sky.

"Swan Maiden," Ava thought.

And then, under her, Helen's body clenched and her wings rose into the air and suddenly the grass was far below them, the moon seemed so close, and they were rising together over the trees.

Ava's hair flew out behind her. The air streamed against her skin. She held on to Helen's neck, and didn't know whether to look up at the moon and stars or down below at the treetops, the curving, gleaming creek, the twinkling lights of the houses, and, farther away, much farther, the town, as she and the swan swam through the sky.

CHAPTER SIX

"*Ava!*"

The banging seeped into her sleep. Over and over and over.

"Ava!!"

She bolted awake.

Sun streamed into the room. She looked at the clock. It was 8 a.m.

"Ava, you're going to be late for school!"

Her head ached. She felt as if she could sleep for hours more.

"Avaaaaaa!"

"Yes, I'm coming," she grumbled. "I'm getting up."

"Since when did you start locking your door? And leaving the gourmet dinners I leave for you in the microwave to rot?"

Since I started growing feathers, she thought, automatically reaching up to feel her upper arms. To her surprise, her arms were smooth. Perfect. Smoother than they'd ever been before.

And then she remembered the clearing and the swans, the beautiful woman, Helen, who'd shown up at the door, who'd taken her flying over the forest . . .

And the spaghetti bolognese. Had she really forgotten to eat her father's famous spaghetti?

Either it was all true, or she'd had one very, very strange dream while, apparently, letting her father's spaghetti rot. Which was really almost the strangest part.

She shook her head, pushing the covers off of her, and looked around the room.

Everything seemed normal. Her window slightly open, the smell of summer blowing in from outside. Flowers and warmth and freshly cut grass. She could hear the sprinkler going off in the backyard. A lawnmower in the distance.

"Ava," her dad called from outside her door, "please do not turn into a sullen teenager on me. Your old dad may not be able to take it."

"Dad, I'm getting ready!"

She leapt up and stared at herself in the mirror. She was normal, perfect. In fact she had never been so happy to see her normal self. So what if her stomach pooched and her upper arms could have been skinnier? So what if she couldn't get a tan? She was completely feather free! Everything *had* been a dream, hadn't it?

A pang of sadness moved through her, a hollowness in her heart and gut, as she remembered the magical woman telling her that her mother was alive, a swan maiden, and that she would be able to see her. Imagine! Her mother with her long moon hair, transforming into a swan. She and her sisters swimming in the creek. Her mother never having really died, just having flown away. It was all so beautiful, but none of it had been real. Had it?

And then suddenly she remembered something else. Under the bed.

Her heart racing, she bent down, lifted the comforter...and there it was. The feathered robe. Ava reached in and pulled it out and spread it over the bed.

The feathers sparkled in the sunlight. Seemed to breathe in and out, as if they were alive. She ran her palms over the robe and the feathers seemed to move into her hands, like before.

She lifted the robe up to her neck, turned and faced the mirror.

Outside, her father banged on the door.

"I don't hear a shower running, kiddo, and it's 8:15!"

"I'm showering right NOW," she said, sighing, shoving the feathered robe into her backpack and stumbling into the bathroom.

Sadly, exploring her magical new swan maiden robe would have to wait.

School always got in the way of things that were important.

Morgan was waiting on the front steps of the school when Ava's father, who was in an unnaturally good mood for some reason, dropped her off.

"No hoodie?" she cried out as Ava approached.

Ava swung her hips from side to side, in an exaggeratedly sexy walk. An Ava Gardner walk. For once in her life she didn't care who was watching. She could just be herself. Let them all laugh if they didn't like it! AVA LEWIS, she imagined, in sparkling lights.

"I am much too fashionable for a hoodie," she said, stretching out her bare arms and flipping her hair. Not only was she not wearing a hoodie, she was wearing a pretty sleeveless blouse and a short skirt rather than her usual jeans and T-shirt.

"Oh my god," Morgan said. "You're... They're gone."

"You look great, Ava," George Kutz said as she walked by.

Out of the corner of her eye, Ava saw Jeff Jackson standing with a group of his friends. She turned and waved, smiling brightly at him.

For some reason, she didn't feel nervous the way she

usually did. She didn't feel nervous at all.

"Ava!" he called out, and he rushed up to her, leaving his friends gaping at them both. Jennifer was there, Ava could not help but note with an unusual feeling of satisfaction. Standing, as usual, with her hands on her hips and that mean-girl look on her face. Ava raised her hand and waved.

"Hey, Jennifer!" she called, smiling as Jennifer lost her cool and looked away awkwardly, not knowing how to respond.

Ava glanced up at Morgan and winked. Her friend raised her eyebrows and both thumbs.

"Dork," Ava mouthed.

She turned to Jeff, who was just walking up to her. "How have you been, Ava?" he asked. He stood towering over her, his head bent down, his blue eyes seeming to crackle like a turning kaleidoscope.

"I was sick for a few days," she said. "I'm sorry if I was kind of a freak at the lake. I didn't know I was sick, but I'm better now."

"You seem better," he said. "You look really pretty." A slight blush spread over his cheeks.

Jeff Jackson—blushing! And calling her pretty! This was definitely the best day of her life, ever.

"Thank you," she said, feeling the blush creep into her own cheeks as well. Why couldn't she be the cool one, just this once?! "How are you?"

"Good," he said. "Will you be at the lake again next weekend, you think?"

"I think so," she said. "I mean, it's summer now. I love it there."

"Me, too." He paused. "Maybe we could get a lemonade again, walk around some."

"Ride the carousel," she said, smiling.

"Yeah. Okay well. So we'll talk more then."

"Sure. That would be great."

He looked down, and then up again. "Okay. Bye."

"Bye."

She watched him walk off, back to his friends. A second later, Morgan was beside her, staring at her with huge green eyes. "Ava Lewis," she said. "You NEED to start returning my text messages."

"Did you see that?"

"Like, the *whole school* saw that," Morgan said. "What did he say?"

"Oh, just that we'll get some more lemonade at the lake next weekend. You know, hang out." She grinned. "Me and Jeff Jackson!"

"He so likes you."

Smiling, Ava looked over again, saw Jennifer and her friends looking her up and down over their shoulders as they headed into school.

They were just trying to intimidate her. What did she

care? Her mother was alive. And her mother was a swan maiden.

"I've got something amazing to show you," Ava said, turning to her friend.

"I just *saw* something amazing, Ava. You and Jeff Jackson! Do you realize what this means? It gives hope to all of us. Anything is possible!"

"Thanks a lot."

"You know what I mean. You're not one of the zombies, and the most popular guy in school is totally into you. It gives us all hope. If you can get Jeff, maybe one day I can get Josh Kirschner."

Ava smiled. Josh had brown hair, dark eyebrows, and the coolest greenish blue eyes, like marbles. He was one of Jeff Jackson's best friends, and Morgan had had a crush on him forever.

"Hey!" she said, a thought occurring to her. "Maybe this year I'll have a really great birthday party and invite them both!"

Morgan looked at her with huge eyes. "Yes! That would be so cool!"

"You have to help me. I want to throw the best party *ever*."

"I have a million ideas already!"

The bell rang, signaling two minutes until homeroom. Immediately, the groups on the lawn broke up, and students from every direction began swarming into the school.

"Hey! Do you notice anything else different about me?" Ava shouted over the crush of students as they headed to the front doors.

"Oh my god, I was so amazed to see you and Jeff I forgot about the whole feathers thing! I mean, I thought you'd blown it, Ava. I really did, between your freaky behavior at the lake and your general freakiness yesterday. Some guys must just like freaks, even handsome popular guys."

It was so typical of Morgan to be more concerned about boys than the most momentous, magical, amazing thing that could ever happen to anyone *ever*.

"Being a freak is underrated," Ava said. "Meet me at lunch and you'll see."

"Like I'm *not* meeting you for lunch. Sorry, I have a date at the beauty salon with my best friend, Jennifer Halverson."

"Jealousy really doesn't suit you, Morgan," Ava said, blowing her friend a kiss and heading to the first class of the day.

She didn't even mind walking into homeroom and possibly trying to face her language arts homework to boot.

There was a first time for everything.

Finally, sitting at her desk, she had a chance to think, about the swans, the woods, her mother. She wondered if her father knew. Had he known all along? Could you marry a swan maiden and not know?

But Ava thought about Helen and Lara and the rest of them, who, no matter how beautiful and extraordinary, looked 100 percent human. If there was a way to pick out a swan maiden in human form, Ava had no idea how.

She her*self* was a swan maiden in human form, and she looked normal, didn't she?

The thought hurtled through her like an arrow. She patted her knapsack, making sure the feathered robe was still there.

She felt the same wonder and disbelief she'd felt the day her father took her to Santa for the first time, when she stared up at the old man in the red suit and imagined him crossing the sky in a sleigh pulled by reindeer. The world had seemed so gigantic then!

And now, suddenly, it felt as if there were things that were even more important than Jeff Jackson (as wonderful and gorgeous as he was!) and Jennifer Halverson and all the zombies and the crowd at the lake. All this was only one tiny sliver in this whole huge world that was filled with magic and wonder.

Who knew what else there was, hidden behind things that seemed totally normal? She looked around at her classmates. What if Vivienne Witmer were secretly…a fairy? Ava studied the girl's long yellow hair that fell over her desk as she sat with her head bent over her book, reading, across the room. She looked at Vivienne's bright purple T-shirt. Could there be little insect wings back there, flat against her back, just waiting to come to life? Maybe the whole mean-girl zombie thing was just a cover.

Ava herself hadn't known about swan maidens a day ago. Who knew what she'd know about tomorrow? Maybe Vivienne Witmer being a fairy was just the tip of the iceberg, as Grandma Kay would say.

She shivered with excitement.

"Ava, eyes to the page!" she heard.

She looked up as Mrs. Holloway stopped in front of her, hovering over her desk. "Ava Lewis, you need to stop that daydreaming for once and focus on the work in front of you!"

Ava could feel herself go red as she mumbled an apology and looked down at her language arts homework.

It really seemed very unfair that she had to do homework, considering the circumstances, but she supposed even swan maidens needed to know how to spell.

At lunchtime, Ava and Morgan met at their usual spot, in the bleachers overlooking the track field.

"I hope you have enough to share," Ava said as Morgan pulled out a thick peanut butter and jelly sandwich. "Last night and this morning were so crazy, I forgot to pack a lunch."

"Fine" Morgan sighed, reluctantly handing half of her sandwich to Ava. "It *must* have been crazy for you to forget about food. I might have to record this moment for posterity."

"Well, I've remembered now," Ava said, taking a huge bite. Morgan's mother made the best sandwiches. Even peanut butter and jelly tasted heavenly when she made it, with jam she canned herself every summer, super crunchy peanut butter, and thinly sliced banana. Once Ava thought she detected a thin layer of honey, too, but she'd gobbled down the sandwich too quickly to be sure.

It was a warm, beautiful day. Students from one of the eighth grade gym classes were running laps around the field and the girls watched them lazily.

"So what's the deal?" Morgan asked. "One day you have feathers and the next day you totally don't?"

"You're not going to believe what I have to tell you."

"Well, let's hear it then!"

"Okay. So the feathers? They peeled off last night. I shed them, like a snakeskin or something disgusting like that. Except they're not disgusting. They're amazing. It's this one long feathered robe."

Ava told Morgan the rest of what had happened the night before. Her friend listened without moving, just staring at Ava with huge eyes until she finished.

"So you haven't put it on yet?" Morgan asked finally.

"No, I haven't had time. Plus, I mean . . . it's a little weird. Right? What if I change and don't change back?"

"I'll still hang out with you," Morgan said. "If that happens, maybe I can borrow that awesome Betsey Johnson dress you got for your birthday?"

"Morgan, get it through your head. You will never wear that dress. Even if I turn into a swan. Not after what you did to that Esprit sweater I loved."

"That was *not* my fault."

"All I know is one day it was perfect, the next it was covered in taco sauce."

"Okay, fine," Morgan said. "If you get stuck as a swan I promise I won't take your Betsey Johnson dress. I'm not sure what you'll do about it if I *do*, but ... "

"Morgan! This is a highly serious matter. I'm a swan maiden. I mean hello. Swan. Maiden."

Morgan sighed. "I *know*. God. *I'm* the one who leaves milk out for fairies and cookies for the elves, but I never see anything. You get magic *and* Jeff Jackson. It's so not fair."

"Well, I don't have him yet."

Morgan rolled her eyes. "Whatever. So. Where IS the robe?"

Ava nodded to her backpack.

"You brought it to school? In your BACKPACK?" Morgan yelled, so loudly that the kids running by right then all turned to stare.

"It's my magic robe, Morgan. I can't just *leave* it somewhere."

"But what if someone steals it from your backpack? Like, then anyone could turn into a swan."

"No, just me."

Morgan's face fell. "Are you sure?"

"Pretty sure. What, you wanted to try?"

"Um. Of COURSE I DO. Have you ever seen a more swanlike creature?" Morgan turned to the side and stretched out her neck. "Look at this grace," she said, pointing at her throat. "I was born to be a swan!"

"Okay, well, you can try. It just . . . You slip it on and become a swan. You pull it off and become . . . a *maiden*, I guess."

"Wow."

"I know."

"Can I see?"

"I'm not pulling it out right here!"

Morgan made an exasperated face, which always made Ava laugh because Morgan's eyes practically popped out of her head like a bug's. "Just open your bag and let me look!"

"Fine," Ava said. And even though she tried to sound annoyed, she too was dying to see the feathers again. As horrifying as they'd been when they were growing on her body, now they were fascinating, wonderful. Like frosted vanilla icing. Like the fur of a polar bear.

Ava reached down and grabbed her backpack.

"Okay, look," she said, unzipping it and placing it on her lap.

Morgan breathed in sharply. "Oh my god," she said.

"What?"

"It's so strange," Morgan said.

"Well. It *is* a magic robe. But what do you mean?"

Morgan reached in her long, freckled fingers, burying them in the feathers. "They just feel so . . . Not just soft, but like. . . It feels like there's a bunny rabbit in here or something, you know? Something alive."

"Well. It sort of is, I guess."

"That's totally weird."

"Well . . . DUH. It's not like I got it at the Gap. Of course it's weird."

Morgan nodded. "Weird and awesome."

Ava shrugged. "Yeah. But . . . "

"But what?"

Ava looked at her friend. "I'm scared! Hello! How could I not be scared? It's freaky!"

"Well. Good things are scary sometimes, right? It's an amazing thing, you know." She looked at Ava, softening. "I mean, you're magic."

"Yeah, I suppose that's true," she said, sighing, as Morgan rolled her eyes. "Will you come over and help me?"

"After school? I'll come to your house?"

"Yes, please," Ava said. Grateful she didn't have to do it alone. She was as terrified as she was exhilarated. The whole future opened up in front of her, filled with possibility. It overwhelmed her.

"Hey," Morgan said "So when will you see the swan

maidens again? And your mom?"

Ava shrugged. "The next full moon."

"Really?"

"That's when they transform, Helen said, so I can't see them until then."

"Oh!" Morgan scrambled for her bag, suddenly excited.

"What?"

"Hold on." Morgan shuffled through her bag and pulled out a miniature calendar, the one her crunchy New Age aunt had given her for Hanukkah the year before. "I noticed something the other day." She unfolded the calendar and scrolled down with her finger. "Yep, I thought so. The next full moon. It's on your birthday!"

"What?" Ava stared at Morgan and then down at the calendar. There it was, the big open circle, smack dab on the Saturday of her birthday. "That's crazy." She felt like her mind was about to explode.

"It's like it's totally meant to be, huh?"

"Yeah," Ava said. "Wow."

"This really *is* going to be the best birthday ever," Morgan said, shaking her head. "So we've got to make your party amazing."

"Yeah."

Ava didn't even know what to say, as she let everything hit her and as she watched, distractedly, as Lynn Johnson huffed and puffed around the track, her black ponytail bobbing up and down.

Morgan grew quiet as well, and the two friends sat side by side, taking in the scene in front of them. The backpack between their feet. Overhead, just then, a flock of birds flew by, squawking and twittering. Everything was strange, hypnotic.

"So you'll really be able to fly," Morgan said after a few minutes had passed.

Ava shook herself out of her reverie. "I guess so. Maybe. The rest of them did."

"Do you think your mom's been watching you? Sometimes?"

Ava's eyes filled with tears. Embarrassed, she wiped them away. "I don't know."

Morgan was obnoxious sometimes, and sometimes downright mortifying to be around, but she did know when to be quiet. She put her arm around Ava and the two of them just sat there, silent, watching the runners in front of them and the birds passing above them, going who knows where, until the bell rang, signaling the end of the period.

CHAPTER SEVEN

*I*n the late afternoon, the woods seemed so innocent and sweet, it was hard to imagine that the night before they'd been full of swans that could transform into maidens and then back again. It was hard to imagine the dark and the moon at all when the sun spilled over the leaves and down to the earth like melted butter.

The leaves flitted around the girls in a soft breeze as they wandered into the forest, following the well-worn trail that led to the creek, the same one her dad took to go fishing. Squirrels scurried up tree trunks. Acorns fell from the trees. The girls had to push back the thin branches, with leaves dangling from them like charms, as they moved along the path.

Ava tried to remember if they'd walked this path last night, she and the swan maiden Helen, but as hard as she tried, she found she couldn't remember. Not the path they'd walked or how long it had taken them to reach the strange clearing. It seemed like every detail, in fact, was out of reach. When she tried to picture the clearing now, all she saw was a pool of water, silver and gleaming, surrounded by trees. She blinked, pushing past a branch as Morgan led them deeper into the woods. But it had been grass drenched in moonlight. Hadn't it?

Everything from the night before seemed like a half memory, something from a dream that slipped away as soon as you woke up no matter how hard you tried to remember. She patted her backpack again to make sure she could feel the bulk within it.

Above them, the sky was bright blue.

Was her mother somewhere, watching that same sky?

Morgan stopped suddenly, under an ancient oak tree with a huge knot in its center. "Look."

"What is it?" Ava walked up to it and peered in.

"I bet an elf lives in here," Morgan said, scrunching up her face to look thoughtful.

Ava was about to tell her she was crazy when she caught herself. "I guess there could be an elf in there, couldn't there?" she said.

"Yes," Morgan said, shrugging.

Ava looked at her friend. Morgan had always believed in magical creatures, she realized, whereas Ava herself had never given them much thought. Of course, it was Morgan's mother who'd read her stories about witches and fairies and mermaids and unicorns, Morgan's mother who had a big herb garden filled with special plants that were supposed to bring you true love or fortune or just plain good luck. As far as Ava could tell, though, if those herbs really worked Morgan should be living in the biggest house in town, not in a sweet little clapboard house where she had to share her bedroom with her annoying younger sister, Fay.

Ava's father had been far too practical to read her stories about fairies and the rest. He had read her stories about Tarzan and the Old West and Al Capone, and pointed out the constellations to her while talking about supernovas and black holes. She was jealous of Morgan, suddenly, even more than she'd been before. Maybe having mothers meant learning about magic, along with everything else. Of course Ava had had Grandma Kay, but that was different.

A mother was something else altogether.

"So I think this is the perfect spot," Morgan said. "No one around for miles."

"Except for an elf or two, maybe."

Morgan waved her hand. "Oh, they don't count."

"I guess not," Ava said, standing there, holding her backpack.

For a minute, neither girl moved. Overhead, a cluster of birds passed, seeming to swim through the air.

"Well?" Morgan said finally, her hands on her hips. "Did you just want to stand here all day staring at the sky?"

"There are worse things to do."

"Yeah, and better," Morgan said, grabbing for the backpack.

"Stop it!" Ava held on tight, but Morgan didn't let go. Suddenly the zipper flew open, both girls stumbled back, there was a terrible ripping sound, and the feathered robe came tumbling out and landed in the dirt.

Ava gasped. Her heart froze in her chest.

The two girls looked at each other.

"Did we . . . break it?" Morgan breathed.

"I don't know." Trembling, Ava dropped down to her knees to touch it. As she reached out her hand, the edge of the robe closest to her seemed to shrink away. Or did she imagine it? She grabbed the robe and pulled it to her, sitting back and gathering it in her lap.

Morgan crouched down next to to Ava, the ends of her long red hair hanging down and scraping the feathers.

Around them, the woods were completely silent, except for the faint faint rushing of creek in the distance.

"Is it okay?" Morgan asked, her voice soft and timid.

"I'm so sorry, Ava."

"I don't know," she said, trying to keep her voice calm.

She stood and held up the robe, tentatively, as if it were made of glass, unfolding it so that it hung down in, almost, one big sheet. Wincing, she held it away from herself so she could see.

It was worse than she thought it'd be. The robe was covered in dirt. Near the center, the feathers were all awry, sticking out in different directions like a bad hairdo. Worst of all, a large rip ran up the bottom.

Ava's heart fell to her knees. She wanted to sob.

"Maybe you should put it on to see," Morgan whispered, finally. "Maybe it doesn't matter."

"Okay," Ava said, unconvinced. She forced herself not to cry, knowing her friend felt bad enough already.

But just as she was about to pull the robe around her shoulders, something happened. A quiet sound, like breathing . . . And then, as both girls watched, the feathers smoothed and whitened and the tear mended, slowly, from bottom to top, until the robe gleamed like a bright white moon in the midst of the pitch black night.

"Did you see that?" Ava asked, barely able to breathe. The robe seemed to shiver under her fingers.

"Yes!"

The girls stared at each other and then at the robe, which hung still now, glowing.

"It's so beautiful!"

"It's amazing," Morgan said. "Oh, Ava, put it on!"

Ava smiled and took a deep breath, her heart pounding with excitement. She pulled the robe around her shoulders. Before she could even put her arms through the sleeves, she felt the robe fusing to her back.

"Oww!"

"Oh my god!" Morgan leapt up. "What's happening?"

But Ava couldn't have answered even if she'd known what to say.

The feathers were like flames running down her back, her arms, and then her body bent and dropped down, her neck stretched up, and suddenly she was close to the ground, warm and strange, peering up at Morgan, who stood over her screaming and flailing about. But Ava could no longer hear her, not the way she could before.

Everything was different. Everything looked different, felt different, smelled different.

The air was different, even.

Ava was sure she could hear the sounds of the creek, the flopping of fish, the hush of the trout moving through the water. How was that possible?

She stretched out her wings. The breeze sifted through them. They lifted on their own accord. Her neck stretched out after them. Above her, Morgan didn't look at all like herself. She was misshapen, stretched out too long and too tall like taffy. Over her, the trees were a dark, glowing green. The sky was like an ocean she could dive into.

Ava laughed. Morgan looked so funny! But what came out was a long, strange honking sound. She laughed again and the air was filled with it.

With each passing second she felt more and more comfortable in her new body. It was so . . . light! And lovely. She stepped forward, flapping her wings, and let out another loud honk when Morgan jumped back, screaming.

"Now turn back!" she heard suddenly, cutting through the haze of other sounds, and she focused again on the strange creature in front of her. "Ava! Turn back into a human!"

And Ava tried to remember . . . But instead all she could think about was how beautiful the sky was. How inviting. And it was so strange, the feeling that she was in the air and the sky was below her.

She realized then that she felt *exactly right*. Perfect. This is how she'd always wanted to feel! Her body, sleek and small and perfect. Weightless. She had imagined that sometimes, how nice it would be to float through the air and have no body at all. And now this, here, was almost like that. She lifted her wings again and flapped them, and the next thing she knew she was *in the air*, her face was level with Morgan's face, and it was easier than being on the ground.

HONKKK!

Right in Morgan's face.

HONK HONK!

She couldn't stop laughing at Morgan's horrified expression, and that only made things worse.

HONK HONK HONKKKKKKKKK!

She was so busy laughing she forgot to move her wings, and then she was flat on the ground with her feet—her fins? what were they?—at her sides, and Morgan was standing over her, swatting at her neck. "Hey, stop that!" Ava called, filling the air with more honking.

"Ava, you change back right now! It's my turn!!!"

Ava focused again on Morgan's words. Change back? Why would she do that, when all she wanted was to launch herself into the air? Why would she change back *ever*? This was so awesome!

And then she remembered that she was a human girl, and that even though she felt awkward and embarrassed all the time—though not today, not now, today she hadn't felt awkward hardly at all, had she, even with Jeff Jackson calling her pretty and all the zombies giving her their mean-girl looks?—she *did* want to see her father and Grandma Kay and her friends, okay, friend, and she wanted to kiss Jeff Jackson and possibly she even wanted to see Monique. Though that was a stretch. Plus, she had an amazing birth-day party to plan.

But she couldn't remember what to do to change back.

She flapped her wings a few times.

She stomped her weird flat feet.

And then she thought about the feathered robe, how she'd slipped it on, and she moved as if she were lifting her hand and reaching for it, not even thinking about what she was doing . . . and suddenly everything happened in reverse and she was standing next to Morgan, the feathered robe in her hand.

She blinked and looked at her friend.

"Oh my god, you almost killed me!" Morgan cried. Ava wasn't listening. A euphoria moved through her. It was as if she'd just arrived at the top of Mount Everest, or ridden a roller coaster so fantastic it hadn't been designed yet. "That was amazing!"

"Well, you are the stupidest-looking swan I have ever seen."

Ava jumped up in the air, and then started bouncing up and down like a pogo stick.

"AND the stupidest-looking human."

Ava stopped bouncing. "Morgan, I cannot possibly explain to you how awesome that was."

"Well, luckily you don't have to," Morgan said, reaching for the feathered robe. She stopped just before her hands touched it. "Can I?"

"Yes, fine," Ava said, though now she regretted having told Morgan she could try it. What if her friend really did ruin it? What if it wasn't allowed?

Morgan's face was shining as she took the robe, and Ava felt suddenly guilty. "Here, I'll help you," she said.

Morgan smiled. Ava stood behind her friend, helping her maneuver into the robe. It was awkward; when Ava had done it, she hadn't even had time to slip her arms through the sleeves before she transformed. With Morgan, the two girls together had to struggle to get her arms through the slightly too-narrow sleeves.

Nothing happened. Morgan stood wearing the robe, but she was definitely still a human girl. "Did I do it right?" she asked, after a minute had passed.

"I think so. Let's try it again."

They slipped the robe off and then on again. Still nothing happened.

"It looks kind of glamorous on you, at least," Ava said. And it did. With her red hair and green eyes, Morgan looked like some kind of exotic Russian queen or something.

Morgan was not soothed. "Maybe we did break it," she said, her voice quivering with disappointment. "Here, you put it on again."

Ava took the robe and slipped it on. Immediately the feathers spread like a fire over her skin and she was back on the ground, stretching out her wings.

"Wooooo!" she yelled. This time, she leapt into the air and fluttered her wings up and up, until she was above the trees looking across the sky. And then she swooped down to the ground, reached back as if she had arms . . . and was standing holding the robe again, shining with joy.

Morgan, on the other hand, was dejected. "I guess it only works on you, huh?"

"I guess so. Last night, one of them said I couldn't use hers, so I figured . . . I'm sorry. But it was worth a try."

"It's so not fair. I'm the one who should be a swan maiden."

"Well, *you* have a mom, at least."

"I have a pretty good mom, don't I?"

"Yeah. So quit being so jealous."

"Well, hopefully soon you'll have a mom, too."

Ava nodded. "Yeah." She smiled. "And if I get a mom? *Then* you can be totally, completely jealous."

"Deal."

The sun was beginning to fall in the sky, and the light grew more dim in the woods. Ava stuffed the robe into her backpack and the two friends made their way out of the forest and to Ava's house.

The house looked so cozy and sweet, in front of them, as they left the woods. Its little chimney jutted into the sky. Ava's dad was already home; the lights were on in the kitchen and living room, and Ava could see him moving around the kitchen.

"Oh no," she said.

"What?"

"You'll see."

The girls burst into the house, which smelled like meat and wine. Monique yowled a greeting and Morgan scooped her up, pressing her own cheek into the cat's.

"Can you take her home with you, please?" Ava asked.

"You are the most glamorous cat in the whole world," Morgan said in her annoying cat voice, ignoring Ava. Monique purred loudly, looking at Ava accusingly.

"Girls!" her father yelled then, coming out of the kitchen. He was wearing a big goofy apron and a chef's hat, and holding a wooden spoon. "I'm making my special veal marsala," he said. "Hungry? You staying for dinner, Morgan?"

"Oh, thank you, Mr. Lewis," Morgan said, suddenly going all bashful, a blush creeping up her pale, freckled cheeks, "I promised my mom I would be home. We're having company tonight."

"Ah, well then, you'll have to have a taste now of my famous red sauce."

"It smells amazing!" Morgan said. Knowing what was coming, Monique jumped out of her arms and scuttled away.

Ava rolled her eyes as they followed her dad into the kitchen, which was now a complete disaster, with pots and pans everywhere and bread crumbs and flour and grated cheese covering the counters.

"Dad!"

"Ava, this is how a real cook works," he said as he dipped his spoon into one of the bubbling pots. "Now behold my famous pasta sauce."

As Morgan leaned in and tasted a spoonful, doing a good job of pretending she hadn't tasted it a thousand times before, Ava suddenly had a memory. Just a flash of one, a sliver: her father and mother standing over the stove laughing together while she played on the floor. Her father feeding her mother a spoonful of something from the stove. Their two heads together, her mother's long moon hair next to her father's dark curls.

"Dad, you cooked this for Mom, too, didn't you?"

He looked at Ava, surprised. "Of course," he said, after a second. "It's my specialty. She loved it."

"It's delicious!" Morgan gushed.

"I remember," Ava said. "I remember you guys cooking together."

He smiled. Handsome despite his ridiculous getup. "Yes," he said. "She liked to cook. She never really had before. We had a lot of fun in this kitchen."

The two girls gave each other a look. Ava felt a strange sort of shiver going down her back.

Her mother, here, over this stove, tasting her father's sauce. But she'd been a swan, she wasn't supposed to have been here at all, Helen had said. A swan maiden, cooking Italian food in this little wooden house. Her mother!

"How come she had never cooked before?" Ava asked. "Isn't that weird?"

Her father shrugged. "She'd always loved being outside so much, your mother, she was a bit of a wild child. I tamed her, in a way. She loved this house, loved cooking in this kitchen, loved you and being your mother."

"Really?"

"Of course. She was madly in love with you. Who wouldn't be?"

Morgan snorted.

"I thought you had to get home," Ava said.

"I'm going! I was just trying some sauce. It's so good, Mr. Lewis, thank you!"

"You're welcome," he said, ruffling Morgan's hair.

Ava knew she wouldn't let anyone else in the world do that to her, but Morgan loved Ava's dad and was always giddy and silly in his presence. He seemed to have that effect on most women, though he never seemed to notice.

"Dad," Ava said, her mind whirling, after her friend had left. Her dad was frying eggplant and veal now, and the kitchen was even more of a mess than it had been before. "How come you don't date anyone ever?"

"Date anyone?" He turned and looked at her, a slice of eggplant in his hand. "Why are you asking me that?"

"Well you're not *that* old, right? And you're sort of good looking."

"Thanks, honey."

"And Mom has been dead for ten years."

"Mmmmhmmm," he said, pulling fried eggplant out of the pan and laying it on some paper towels.

"She is dead, right?"

He stopped what he was doing, turned down the burner, and leaned back against the counter. "Ava," he said, looking at her intently, "why are you asking me that? You're not experimenting with drugs are you? Let me see your pupils."

"How did you meet, anyway? You never told me how you guys met."

"I haven't?"

"No, Dad! You never talk about her!"

He looked so sad for a moment that Ava almost wished she hadn't asked. His shoulders sagged, and his face, so handsome, seemed to break open.

"Dad—" she started.

"No, I should talk more about her to you," he said. He looked far away then, his face softening as he remembered. Ava watched him, barely breathing, afraid to break the spell.

"Are you okay?" she asked.

He nodded. "It was summertime, and I was down by the creek with my rod. The fish back then practically jumped into your hands. It was twilight. There was a great big full moon, I remember, just peeking out. And then I saw a woman swimming in the creek with her friends and I'd never seen anyone more beautiful, not even in the movies, or in the magazines, or in my dreams."

"Then what?" she asked.

He shrugged. "We started talking. I don't remember all the details. I knew right away I would marry her. And that was that. There's someone for each of us, Ava, and your mother was the one for me."

"Do you ever think about her now?" Ava asked.

He sighed. "Of course I do. I think of her every day. And I see her every day, in you."

"Really?"

"Yes, really. You're so much like her. It scares me sometimes, seeing you become so like her. You look more and more like her every year, too, even with that black hair. You even walk like she did. The same voice, everything. And now you're about to be a teenager. I can't believe it."

Ava felt tears prickling at her eyes. "How come you've never told me that?"

He shrugged. "I thought I had."

And then he turned around and fired up the burner again, absorbing himself in the veal and the eggplant. But before he did, Ava was sure she saw tears prickling in his eyes, too.

CHAPTER EIGHT

ver the next few days, Ava focused more on her birthday party than anything else. She and Morgan made up a list of kids to invite that started out small and ended up including practically the whole seventh grade, even Becky Rainer with her greasy hair and Jennifer Halverson and her crew. It didn't feel right to exclude anyone, and she figured no zombie would set a pedicured, kitten-heel-wearing foot in her house anyway. The girls planned out a menu, which Ava's father approved instantly as it featured his famous meatballs and spaghetti as well as Ava's (and his) favorite dessert, a pistachio ice-cream cake with Heath bars crumbled across the top.

Ava had never had a party before, and certainly not one on such a momentous occasion as her thirteenth birthday and in her very own house to boot. Before, even just a week ago, she would have been mortified at the idea of letting her classmates into the quaint little house with the wraparound porch and the basement full of handmade fishing rods, and she would have cringed at the idea of being the center of attention. She would have been terrified that no one would come or, if they did, that they would discover some new dorky thing about her that she'd forgotten to hide. But something big had changed since she started growing feathers, she realized, and she didn't have the same twisty feeling in the pit of her stomach when imagining a room full of her classmates in her own house. It would be fun. If anyone didn't like her house or her stuff or her cool professor dad with his salt-and-pepper hair and love of the Rolling Stones and fly fishing, it was, really, their loss.

She tacked up a ballerina calendar on the wall and started marking down the days. And that Friday night she counted down: just twenty-nine days until her birthday, her party, and the next full moon.

She woke up the next morning feeling wild with excitement. On top of everything else, there were only two more weeks of school left before the long summer, which stretched out in a perfect, blissful haze with no school, no getting up before eight in the morning, just whole days at the lake and in the mountains. She wanted to jump up and down with excitement, thinking about the future. Becoming a teenager, going to the high school in another year, going to college, moving to a big city like New York and maybe working for a magazine, or being a famous artist, or opening a little store filled with candy cigarettes and jewelry made from orange slices.

And, of course, finding her mother, and learning about the swan maidens. That future stretched out in front of her, too, a sequence of full moons, waning and waxing and waning again. That's how it worked, right? No matter how tiny the moon became, it always became full again.

She stretched happily, twisting under the covers. Monique flew off the bed and landed on the floor.

"Oh, sorry," Ava said, as Monique turned to her with an outraged expression.

But she couldn't stop smiling. She picked up the photo of her mother by the side of her bed, traced the lines of her mother's face. The new memory, of her mother and father cooking over the stove, stayed with her like a gift, and she clung to it, rolled it over again and again in her mind.

She must have been a baby, playing on the floor, with her parents laughing above her, the kitchen smelling like garlic and onion and frying things. Her mother had liked cooking, her father had said. How strange and wonderful it must have been for her, living in this house, being a human woman, having a child.

Had it been hard for her to leave? Had she missed her other life? Did she miss this life, now?

And if she was really alive, where was she?

She closed her eyes and imagined: riding over the treetops with her mother the way she had with Helen, leaning down and holding her mother's swan body, her fingers burrowing into soft feathers, her mother's wings stretched out and flapping on either side. Feeling her mother's heart beating under her fingertips.

Or: the two of them, flying next to each other, her mother leading her to another, better world. Or up into the stars and to the moon, where Ava had watched for her so many nights. The two of them, flying past stars whirring in the sky beside them, passing through black holes, sliding down the Milky Way . . .

Her phone buzzed loudly.

"Yesss??!!" she answered, knowing it was Morgan, making her voice as goofy as possible.

"Um. Ava?" It was a boy's voice.

Her mouth dropped open. She sat up in bed. "This is Ava," she said, trying to sound normal.

"This is Jeff."

"Jeff?" she repeated.

"Um. Jeff Jackson?"

"Oh. This is Ava."

"I know. I called you."

"Oh." She caught herself. She was the new Ava here, not the old one. She just had to remind herself. "I mean, hey. How are you?"

"Great. I'm just . . . wondering if you were planning to meet me at the lake today?"

"Sure," she said, smiling into the phone. Grandma Kay always said you could hear a smile. "Yes."

"I thought maybe we could go together? Ride our bikes?"

"Oh! Together?"

"Yeah. I could come by your house?"

"Okay."

"Maybe in an hour?"

"Okay."

"Okay. Bye."

"Bye."

She stared at her phone in disbelief, as if it had just grown a mouth and started talking to her all on its own.

Then it hit her, and she screamed. Jeff Jackson was coming to her house! "Oh my god!!!" she cried.

A second later, her father appeared in her doorway. "What's going on?" he asked, his voice and face panicked. "Are you all right?"

"Yes!" She bounded off the bed and leapt across the room and into his arms. "Dad!!! Jeff Jackson just called me!

He's coming here in an hour!"

"Who's Jeff Jackson?"

"Only the love of my LIFE," she said, pulling back and giving him her most serious expression.

"Well, that's great. I was hoping to have a few more years before this kind of thing came up, but . . ."

"Dad, I'm about to turn THIRTEEN. I'm practically an adult."

"Ava, you are not even close to being an adult yet. What are you and this Jeff Jackson planning to do together, if I may ask, only being your father and sole caretaker?"

She rolled her eyes. "We're riding our bikes to the lake."

"Ah." He scratched his chin and pretended to contemplate. "That means I don't have to give you a ride, doesn't it?"

"Yes."

"Well, that sounds like an excellent plan. I like this Jeff Jackson fellow already." He pointed his finger at her. "But ride carefully and make sure you have your phone with you."

"I will, Dad."

"And call me when you get there."

"Okay. I have to get ready!"

He sighed. "Maybe we can order a pizza tonight and you can tell me all about it. I'll spend the day emotionally preparing myself."

"Sure," she said, pushing him out of her doorway. "Now let me get ready!!!"

She shut the door and turned back to her room, and stopped.

Everything was so . . . lovely all of a sudden. The sun shining in through the windows, split by the tree branches outside. The perfume smell of the flowers in full bloom along the side of the house. Her sweet white bed and pink pillows and there, out of sight, under her bed, the feathered robe that seemed to fill the room even when she couldn't see it. The black-and-white photo of her mother. Her computer screen blinking with messages from her best friend, who was really very lovable despite being incredibly annoying. And the pretty sundress hanging on her closet door right next to her new bathing suit.

It was summer. Her thirteenth birthday was in less than a month.

And she was a SWAN MAIDEN.

Ava slipped into the bathing suit and the sundress, which was an off-white cotton with ropy lace around the edges. She turned to the mirror and for the first time in forever wasn't even partially horrified by what she saw: herself, standing there, her long black hair cascading down dramatically against the pale fabric, the way it did against the white feathers of her robe. Her fair skin looked okay to her now. She kind of even liked it. It was who she was. Ava Lewis. Tall and pale, with black hair, twelve years old. And even if everyone loved Jennifer Halverson and the other zombies with their tan skin and blond hair—okay and the one black zombie, Barb Freeman, who looked like Tyra Banks—it was also true that Jeff Jackson, Morgan, and a bunch of swan maidens liked her just the way she was.

Jeff Jackson!

She screamed again and checked the clock. Now that she was ready, the half hour she had left seemed like an eternity.

She sat down in front of her computer then and typed an IM to Morgan: "Jeff Jackson on his way HERE NOW! We're biking to the lake!"

"OMG" came flashing back onto her screen.

"I KNOW!"

"HOW AM I GONNA GET 2 THE LAKE?"

Ava moaned. She'd forgotten all about her plans with Morgan, of course. She was just like one of those lame girls in one of those cheesy teen movies, dropping everything the moment a boy came around.

"I'm sorry," she typed, adding in a stupid unhappy face emoticon. "Can't your mom take u?"

"NO SHE'S WORKING!"

"But it's a date!"

Ava's phone rang. "Ava!" Morgan's voice cried out, as Ava opened the phone several inches from her ear, knowing what was coming. "You cannot do this to me."

"Morgan, this is my first date with Jeff Jackson!"

"But we had plans! And I need to see Josh Kirschner,

who by the way said I looked nice yesterday, which you would have known if you weren't all obsessed with boys and swans and actually cared about your BEST FRIEND for once."

"Oh." Ava felt totally guilty all of a sudden. She *had* been a little selfish, hadn't she? But it wasn't every day that a girl discovered she was a swan maiden. Was it?

But she had been ignoring Morgan a little.

And Josh Kirschner was *almost* as cute as Jeff Jackson with those marble eyes, and Morgan had only been in love with him for five thousand years.

She sighed. "Okay, fine. We can all ride our bikes together."

"I'll be there in a few," Morgan said, and hung up the phone.

Ava sat at her desk, dejected. From this angle, she could see the robe winking and glittering at her from under the bed. Despite herself, she went over to pick it up. Without even thinking she wrapped it around her shoulders and there, in front of the mirror, watched as her body turned to feathers, swooping down into the graceful perfect shape of a swan.

She walked over to the mirror on the closet door, planting one black webbed foot in front of the other. Her black eyes staring back at her. Her feathers like fresh-fallen snow, the way it sparkled under streetlamps and made Christmas—and Hanukkah, for Morgan, her *extremely annoying* best friend— the most magical holiday of the whole year, even better than

Halloween when she got to dress as a mermaid or a cat.

Everything looked more sparkling through these eyes, actually. Her bedspread and computer, the sunlight coming in through the window, the photo of her mother. It was the same room, but entirely different.

She lifted her wings, admiring their curve and shape. What a magical body she had! Even the human things seemed magical now: the way her body told her when it was hungry and when it was tired, the way she bled once a month, the way she was changing, and growing, and becoming a woman . . .

Suddenly, she caught something out of the corner of her eye. Her mother's photo was *really* different now, she realized, more than everything else. She walked up closer to it, craning her long long neck.

It wasn't just her mother leaning against a tree anymore, smiling into the camera, the way it had been for as long as she could remember.

Now Ava could clearly see that her mother was wearing a robe in the photo, one just like hers, the white feathers flaring up around her face like a boa, or waving hands. The photo wasn't misshapen the way other things were—the bed longer and thinner, the computer screen larger and more glaring. Her mother just stood there, staring at her, with the white robe hanging from her shoulders. And she was smiling eerily, as if she were actually looking right at Ava. Her eyes black and glittering.

"Mama," Ava breathed, though what came out was a strange cooing noise.

Her mother's face softened, came into focus, and then there was nothing eerie about it at all. It was as if her own mother were right there. Soft, beautiful, in full color now, her hair a pale creamy gold, her cheeks pink and milky, and around her, bright green leaves and swaying grass.

"Ava." The voice whispered in her ear, was all around her.

"Mama," she repeated. "Please come back."

And then, faintly, just as her mother appeared to move, to walk toward her, she heard the doorbell ringing, cutting through her reverie.

A few seconds later, her father was banging on her door. "Ava!"

She flapped her wings, panicked, almost forgetting herself. And then she reached back and was standing in her room with the robe in her hand, wearing her bathing suit and sundress.

Quickly, she stashed the robe away, stealing a glance up at her mother's photo as she did.

It was the same as before: black and white, her mother in a pale dress, standing against a tree.

There was magic all around her, she realized—things she couldn't see with her regular, human girl eyes.

"Ava!" her father called. "There is a *boy* here for you!"

A burst of happiness moved through her even as she groaned at her father's embarrassingly loud voice. She felt a warmth inside her that she'd never felt before, knowing her mother was so close. A full, glowy kind of feeling, as if the moon itself were inside of her. And it was the moon that would bring her mother to her. The next full moon, she was sure of it.

But for now?

Her one true love awaited.

Before she stepped out into the front hall, where her father stood no doubt regaling Jeff Jackson with the most embarrassing moments of her short-yet-embarrassment-filled life, Ava paused in the living room to lean against the wall and collect herself. *Ava Gardner*, she thought, breathing in, imagining how Ava Gardner would glide into the hallway and toss her hair and flick her eyes down and then up again before saying, "It is such a *pleasure* to see you, Jeff."

And of course he would look at her in amazement, barely able to stammer about how marvelous she looked in her fashionable new swimsuit and sundress.

She took a deep breath, smiled broadly, and stepped into the hallway.

He was so cute! Jeff Jackson stood there all tall and yellow-haired and manly and dimpled, talking with her dad about his *career ambitions*.

"I plan to get a PhD, too, sir," he was saying, and she just about died, he was so adorable.

"It's a good life," her father said, and he would have said more except that Ava, in a misguided attempt to both toss her hair and glide toward her date, tripped on the slick tile and nearly landed in Jeff's arms, just as Morgan burst through the front door, pushing it so that it smacked Jeff Jackson right in the back.

"Girls, girls!" Ava's dad said, just to make things even more totally humiliating. "I know he's handsome but don't *throw* yourselves at the poor kid."

Steadying herself, Ava was about half a second from running to her bedroom in tears when she realized that Jeff Jackson was laughing. Laughing! And not at all in a mean way, either! And then Ava's dad was laughing, and Morgan was laughing, and before she knew it Ava was laughing, too, and by the time Ava, Morgan, and Jeff headed out to the garage to get Ava's bike, the ice had been broken and Jeff didn't even seem to mind that Ava had asked—been *forced* to ask, that is—Morgan along.

It was weird to think that the cutest, most popular boy in school could feel like a friend, too, like a normal kid, but that's how it felt as the three of them biked to the lake, talking and laughing and being total, complete dorks. Morgan even started snorting in her totally embarrassingly dorky way and Jeff did it back to her.

"Oinkkkk!"

Ava pedaled along happily, watching Jeff as he sped ahead and then looked back at her, laughing, urging her forward. She shrugged, looking away, pretending to ignore him, and then suddenly burst forward and shot past him.

"Cheater!" he cried out, zooming up alongside her, and they raced side by side, laughing wildly, as Morgan screamed behind them.

They were at the lake before Ava knew it, and she thought how long the ride in her father's car usually seemed, because the girls were so anxious to get out of the car and onto the beach. Now, with the three of them together, she didn't care if they ever arrived at the lake. For all she cared, they could ride like this all day long.

Once the three were lying on their towels in the sun, side by side, Ava trying not to die of embarrassment every time she looked at Jeff with his naked chest, she told Jeff about her birthday party plans, secretly afraid that he would laugh at her and refuse to come and even, possibly, leave the country to be as far away as possible.

"So you'll come, maybe?" she asked.

"We're going to make it the best party ever!" Morgan said.

"It sounds awesome," Jeff said, turning to Ava and smiling right at her, his big blue eyes even bluer in the sun. "Of course I'll come! I can't wait."

For the rest of the day, as they swam and rode the carousel

and bought hot dogs at one of the vendor stands next to the carousel and ignored—and delighted in—the zombies' horrified, shocked looks, Ava played those three words over and over in her head, spoken in the lovely low voice of her extremely handsome friend and possibly boyfriend (!!!) Jeff Jackson: *I can't wait.*

Neither could she.

CHAPTER NINE

Ava spent all that evening, and all the next day, in a boy-crazed stupor. She couldn't stop thinking about Jeff Jackson . . . smiling, imagining his manly chest under the sun, his yellow hair, what it would be like to kiss him . . .

She couldn't concentrate on anything at all. She tried picking up the vampire novel she was reading, but the words blurred in front of her and instead she saw Jeff Jackson standing there, gazing at her with those crackling blue eyes of his. "Ava," he whispered. "You're so beautiful you make my eyes ache."

She tried watching television but then there he was

sliding next to her on the couch, reaching for her hand, telling her that he'd loved her for as long as he could remember and thought she was the smartest and coolest girl in the whole school.

More than once her father caught her smiling to herself, and asked her what was making her act so goofy. "It's that boy, isn't it?" he'd say. "Do you want to talk about it?"

"No!"

How embarrassing!

But she couldn't even concentrate on the old Greta Garbo movie her dad put on that evening, and spent the whole time staring into space.

"So I'm guessing you had a nice time at the lake with that young man," her father said, sighing and turning off the television.

"It was okay," she mumbled. She turned away from the imaginary Jeff sitting next to her.

"I was hoping you'd be more like . . . thirty when this happened."

"Dad!"

"Well, he is obviously quite enamored of you, too. He looked at you like you were made out of chocolate. And you, my child, you just cannot stop smiling."

"Dad, can you just put the movie back on?"

"Fine," he said, sighing.

But by Sunday morning, she started to worry. Shouldn't he have called her by now?

She lay on her bed, going over everything they'd talked about. Like the way she'd told him she planned to have lots of adventures when she grew up, and wanted to travel all over the place, maybe even to Thailand or California.

Her heart dropped. Panic spread through her, like water being poured over her body and soaking her right through. Maybe he thought she was a hippie!

Morgan told her she was being crazy. "You just saw him yesterday," she said, when she called late that morning. "He *obviously* likes you. It was a little revolting, to be honest."

"Really?"

"Yes! He had this stupid look on his face the whole time we were at the lake, and so did you. I'm getting queasy just thinking about it."

But Ava was inconsolable. "Then why isn't he calling? If he liked me he would want to talk to me."

"Quit being ridiculous. Get on your bike and meet me. Come on, it's amazing out today. Jeff's probably at the lake already."

"Probably sitting with all his friends, laughing about me."

Morgan groaned into the phone. "Can you please just get over here?"

"No, I'm staying home today."

"What?"

"I went to the lake with you yesterday *even though* I had a date. And now he hates me. I'm not going back there— maybe not ever!"

She threw herself on her bed dramatically, hitting her chin on the phone and accidentally hanging up on Morgan.

What did it matter, anyway? Morgan clearly didn't understand that her life was ruined. What was the point of discussing it?

Ava spent the rest of the day in front of the television, to her father's dismay— "you'll rot your brain!" he said, before disappearing into the basement—and by Sunday night she was convinced that Jeff Jackson had never liked her at all and that the whole thing had been a joke, like when Ian Franklin asked out Beth Miller. She could see it so clearly she was convinced she'd turned psychic: him sitting there with all his friends, laughing.

She sat on the couch watching *Jeopardy*, tears streaking her face. She didn't even know any of the answers! In disgust, she finally turned off the television and went to bed, not even bothering to find her dad to say good night.

No one would ever love her, she realized. She would die alone and unloved. Neighborhood children would tell each other stories about the crazy old lady living by herself and occasionally turning into a swan.

She lay on her bed, tears streaming down her face.

Suddenly, there was a rapping on her window. A moment later, her phone rang.

Ava groaned. Why couldn't Morgan leave her alone in her misery, let her suffer in peace?

Her phone buzzed again and she looked down now, saw JEFF JACKSON splayed across it like an old-time chanteuse spread across a grand piano.

"Oh my god!" she shouted out loud, sitting up straight in her bed.

"Ava?" she heard, from outside the window. The voice seemed to be coming from outside, from the bushes.

And it was . . . not a girl's voice.

Before she could stop herself, Ava screamed.

Was it possible for an almost-thirteen-year-old to have a heart attack, she wondered. Or just die from shock?

Quickly, she wiped her face, horrified by the thought of how awful she must look.

"Hello?" she said, her voice squeaking into the phone.

"Hey, Ava," she heard, both from the phone and from the world outside her window. He was right outside.

She stretched up her neck and looked out, saw the top of Jeff's head under the tree, lit up in the moonlight like a suspended halo.

"Are you there?" she heard again. "Ava?"

She ducked down and whispered into the phone. "Jeff, are you outside my window right now?"

"I've come to get you. Let's have an adventure!"

"Right now?"

"Yes! You said you wanted to have adventures, right? Let's have one now! The mayflies are out, the green drakes. We can go down to the creek and watch them."

She held the phone away from her and looked at the time. It was 9:08 p.m.!

What a dork she must seem like, being in bed at 9:08 p.m.

"Umm, okay," she said, her heart pounding in her chest. "Let me, ummm . . . " She was about to say "get dressed" when she realized that he'd know then that she was in her pajamas. A pink nightshirt with three pigs across the front of it, to be exact. "Just give me a few minutes," she started again. "I'll meet you outside."

She hung up the phone and was about to let out a groan when she remembered where he was.

Could she possibly be more of a dork?

But then there was a glimmer, through her pain and embarrassment, and it hit her: JEFF JACKSON WAS GOING TO TAKE HER ON AN ADVENTURE!!! Even if it apparently involved insects, it was still unbelievably romantic.

She jumped up and then slinked over to her closet, in the dark, to grab a sundress, going for the bright white one since it was the only one she could make out.

Scrunching down to make sure he couldn't see—

even though she knew it was too dark and he was too far down...and even if he weren't, Jeff Jackson was totally a gentleman and would never spy on her as she changed her clothes. Would he?

She grabbed the dress and ran to the bathroom, where she clicked on the lights and faced herself in the mirror. Her eyes were puffy and red and her face was all blotchy from crying. She pulled off the nightshirt and slipped into the white dress, which only made her face look more mottled... Ava sighed. At least her hair looked striking against the white fabric, and it *was* dark outside. And the longer Jeff Jackson stood on her lawn, the more possible it was her father would see him and ground her *forever*. He was a pretty cool guy, for a dad, but she *was* sneaking out of the house at night to be with a boy and no dad was a fan of that.

Ava crept out of the bathroom and into the dark house, stopping to listen for sounds. She heard some shuffling from downstairs, from her father's workroom, where he was almost assuredly making more fishing rods for some unfathomable reason. Still, he was safely occupied. Making sure she had her key, she rushed out into the night, locking the front door behind her.

He was standing there on the lawn, smiling. Behind him the sky spread out like a liquid, a sea, and across it were a million stars. The houses hulked up in shadow, like silent monsters, and a breeze moved over the grass and ruffled her hair. It was perfect, the neighborhood at night, with Jeff Jackson standing on her lawn and his blond hair lit up like a halo.

"Hi," she whispered, stepping toward him.

"Hi."

He looked different from the way he did at school, standing there on the lawn, his face soft and even shy as he looked at her.

Suddenly she was shy, too, and for a long moment they just stood and looked at each other.

Jeff cleared his throat. "So...have you ever watched the mayflies before?"

"Umm, no," she said. She paused awkwardly. "What is there to watch?"

"Oh!" he said. "It's amazing! They come out just a few days a year, you know, to mate and then die. The males move up and down, spinning and dancing and swarming together, and the females fly through the swarms and they clasp together and then the males drop into the water and die, and the females lay their eggs on the water and they die, too."

Ava just stared at Jeff, shocked. His face was shining as he spoke, his hands were in the air, and even though it was all totally disgusting it seemed totally romantic to her, too, the way he talked about it.

"And that's all happening now?" she asked.

"Yes. Any time now."

She remembered him mentioning something about this stuff at the lake the day before, she realized, but she had blocked it out.

"That sounds...nice," she said, and his face lit up. His happiness made her blush, and she was grateful for the darkness. She thought she might be dreaming, it was all so strange. Could this shy, lovely boy really be Jeff Jackson?

He reached out and took her hand, and she just about fell over.

"Come on," he said.

She nodded, unable to speak, and let him lead her to the sidewalk. He laced his fingers through hers and she was surprised by how natural it felt. Chills moved up and down her body.

"I know the best spot. I like to watch without crowds of fishermen around."

"My dad's a fly fisherman," she said.

"Really? He must be into the green drakes."

"I don't know," she said, trying to remember her dad talking about this stuff. "He's more into the moon, I think. He always fishes under the full moon."

She couldn't believe they were actually talking ... while holding hands! She couldn't believe she hadn't just fainted dead away from shock. But it actually felt really nice, and even comfortable.

"That's cool," Jeff said. "I'm more into the bugs than the

fish. People say the trout here are smart, but I think the bugs are way more interesting."

"Yeah," she said, trying to sound as if she semi-agreed, even though she didn't agree even slightly.

They walked down the dark street, under the stars and streetlamps, passing out of her neighborhood and through the park where the school had its picnic every year, and past the old playground with the see-saw and the merry-go-round. Mostly they walked in silence, and it was a comfortable silence, like when she and her dad sat at the dinner table and she was happy just to be with him.

As beautiful as the night was, Ava could barely focus on anything other than his hand clasped in hers, the way their arms swung together as they moved. Now and then he turned to her and smiled, his eyes bright with excitement, and she thought that maybe this was the happiest she'd ever been.

Finally, Jeff turned down a narrow path that led back to the creek. The same creek that ran behind her house, in the woods, but farther upstream. She could hear the whooshing of the water rushing by.

"Look!" he said, as they approached the water. He pointed, and she saw white, winged bodies whirring through the air. "They're dancing!"

"Dancing?"

The insect bodies glowed in the pale moonlight, flickering up and down over the water.

"To attract their mates."

Ava smiled, watching the mayflies, and Jeff's face. She realized how special it was, that he'd wanted her to see this even if it was sort of gross and it seemed extremely likely that one of the giant flies would land in her hair.

"Thank you," she said, and he turned to her, that grin on his face that he wore as he walked down the hall at school, like he knew how much everyone admired him.

"I thought you'd like it," he said. "It only happens once a year." He shrugged. "I mean, I know not everyone would be into this, but you just have always seemed ... different."

Her heart skipped a beat. "Different?"

"Yeah," he said, watching her. "You're different. Quiet, like you're always thinking or dreaming about something, and I always wonder what it is."

"Oh."

His face was so soft as he looked at her. He squeezed her hand and she could barely breathe.

In front of them, the flies' white bodies moved over the water.

"Are they really dancing?" she asked.

"Yes," he said. "Watch them. Do you see how they're moving?" He stepped closer to her, pointing with his free hand.

She focused in, and tried to see them as beautiful, through Jeff's eyes, to think about this one moment they had, dancing over the water to attract their mates. They seemed to slow down as she watched, as if the air were thickening, and then she *saw* it. The way they drifted up and down. Enjoying this one moment when they were set loose and free in the air. She thought about the swan maidens standing in the moonlight holding their feathered robes, and suddenly the whole world seemed so full she thought she would explode.

"I see it," she whispered.

"Ava," he said then, his voice cracking.

She nodded, encouraging him. Her heart was pounding so loudly she was sure he could hear it. "Yes?"

"I really like you."

She breathed in. "I like you, too."

"I have for a long time, you know."

"You have?"

"Yeah." He smiled his adorable lopsided smile. "Even when you were a super dork, I thought you were really cute. I mean, you're cute now, too. I like you however you are."

Her eyes dropped to the ground, she was so embarrassed, knowing her cheeks were flaming red. At least it was dark.

"And I like how you blush," he said.

"Hey!" she said, annoyed he could see her blushing in the moonlight. "You blush, too!"

"I know!" he said. "I'm not making fun of you. I just like you."

"Well," she said. "Being obsessed with bugs is pretty dorky, too."

"What do you mean?" he asked, pretending to be shocked.

She laughed, and then when she saw how he was looking at her, she stopped. For a moment, she wondered if he'd kiss her, and she just wanted to slow this moment down, freeze it like a photograph, so she could really appreciate it. It was weird how you could wait and wait for something and then, when it happened, or was about to happen, it passed by in a flash.

But then a splishing sound came from the water, very faint.

Jeff stepped forward, releasing her hand. "Did you see that fish jumping?"

She let out a deep breath, equal parts relieved and disappointed.

"No," she said.

"There's another one! They see the mayflies. It's the best time for fishing, this time of the year."

"So you spend a lot of time here, don't you?"

"Yeah," he said. "I love it here. Especially this part of the creek. All the fishermen hang out more upstream, at least most of them do. Though I bet you could catch a ton of fish here right now."

"Yeah," she said.

They were standing quietly, watching the activity over the water, when Ava noticed one, two swans in the air above them.

"Look," she said, gesturing to the birds.

"That's weird. I don't think I've ever seen a swan over here."

The swans swooped down by the side of the stream. Their eyes black and glittering.

"They're watching us," he said, surprised. "Do you see that?"

"Well, swans are very nosy, you know."

She laughed and gave him a goofy look, as if she were joking. But she was well aware that one of the swans was very likely her mother, or at least a friend of her mother's, which was surely a disadvantage to being the daughter of a swan maiden sneaking out of the house at night with a boy. She glared at them.

"I guess they like watching the mayflies dance, too," he said.

"I guess."

She forced herself to relax. It was all so beautiful: the half-moon, the shining water, the mayflies dancing as the swans glittered behind them, on the grass. Jeff Jackson reaching for her hand again. And even if her mother was a swan who possibly lacked any respect for her daughter's privacy, it was pretty amazing to have a mom after all this time.

Jeff turned and smiled at her. "We better get home, huh?"

"Yeah," she said.

They walked slowly back, through the park and onto her

street, past all the sleeping houses, until they stood together on the lawn in front of her house, their hands laced together.

"Only two more weeks of school," he said, after an awkward silence. "I can't wait for summer. Will you be here?"

"Yes," she said. "I'll be here. My dad's not really the vacationing type, he's too attached to this place." She paused, nervous. "Will you be here?"

"Yeah. So I hope we can do some fun stuff together."

She looked up at him. "I would like that," she said.

"Good."

They stood for another minute, the moments stretching out and seeming to last forever, until finally he said, "I'll go, then."

"Umm, okay," she said.

And then he raised her hand to his mouth, and kissed it, keeping his eyes on hers the whole time.

Her stomach flip-flopped, as if there were a fish trapped inside. She couldn't help breaking out into a huge grin, and had to stop herself from giggling like a dork. "Thank you for the adventure," she said, "and the mayflies."

"Any time," he said. "So, see you at school?"

"Yeah."

She waited until she was inside, and until she was sure that Jeff Jackson was no longer lurking outside her window. And then she threw herself onto her bed, buried her head in her pillow, and screamed with that crazy kind of happiness that feels exactly, perfectly right, like a brand-new dress made just for you.

CHAPTER TEN

*T*he next morning, Jeff Jackson waited for Ava on the school steps, and then he did it the next morning and the next. That weekend, he biked with her and Morgan to the lake, and it was just as natural as it'd been before, as if they'd all been friends for years. Jeff was sweet, funny, kind—so much so that Ava sometimes forgot how handsome he was. Well, until he looked at her with those blue eyes and made her knees go weak, just as Grandma Kay had told her a boy would do someday. And as the entire seventh grade class at Houghton Middle School readied themselves for their final tests, and for the long summer that would follow, it became common knowledge that Ava Lewis and Jeff Jackson were "going together."

The only thing more exciting than that for Ava was her impending birthday. Every morning she slashed through another box on her calendar, counting down. Every day she and Morgan added another cool thing to the party planning, and Morgan even started carrying around a notepad and clipboard to organize the different aspects of the day: food, party favors, guests, music, activities. The coolest thing was Ava's dad getting inspired one night to dust off his ancient banjo and recruit a few friends to provide music for the party. The guys came over twice to practice before the big day, and Ava hadn't seen her dad laugh so much in . . . well, forever. One guy, another professor from the university, played the fiddle, and another, someone her dad knew from his music days, played the accordion. Sure, it was old-people music, but it was fun and sweet and Ava loved those rare occasions when her dad loosened up and got lost in his playing. Way back when, she knew, he'd played soft music as Ava's mother rocked her to sleep, or so he told her. Plus Ava secretly thought the accordion was cool—covered in rhinestones and shiny mother-of-pearl, like a big jewelry box.

Between Jeff and tests and her birthday, Ava was so busy, in fact, that she stayed in her human form until one night, unable to sleep, she decided that maybe, finally, she would try to fly.

It was about a three-quarter moon, but the night was clear and star-speckled as she lay on her back in her bed with her arms bent behind the pillow. In the moonlight, the tree branches silvered. The leaves were shaped like hearts, and she could just make out a bird's nest in the shadows. The branches swayed back and forth in the faint breeze, but it was still hot, one of those hot summer nights when the fan wasn't enough to keep cool and Monique stalked about the house swatting at things.

Ava wiggled closer to the window, leaning against the wall to stare up at the sky, breathing in the perfume from the flowers.

She wondered where the swan maidens were right now. Maybe they had nests, too? She imagined how big and elaborate a swan's nest would have to be for one of them to sleep in it. If *she* had a nest, she thought, she would like a beautiful, fancy one, like an accordion, scattered with rhinestones and mother-of-pearl and maybe shells, too. She imagined the whole lot of them with such nests, adorned and glittering, all the swan maidens fast asleep at this very minute, maybe in some enchanted clearing somewhere or in the branches of some oversized, magical tree.

She shifted, moving her arms down, and folded her hands across her belly. Maybe, instead, they were all off flying somewhere right now, all the swans in a big group—a flock, like a flock of geese? a murder, like a murder of crows?—

sailing through the clouds and stars. Were there other girls out there, riding on the backs of swans? Other daughters of swan maidens nearing their thirteenth birthdays?

She laughed. Really, anything was possible, wasn't it?

And then Ava felt something she'd never felt before, not the way she did then: the desire to fly. A feeling that came up straight from her blood and bones, seizing her like hunger, like love. Her whole body bristled with it. She needed to fly!

She jumped out of bed then. Restless. Crazy. Moonstruck? She reached down to grab the feathered robe, and then hurried through the house with the robe in her arms, and out the sliding glass door, into the backyard. Within seconds she was stretching her wings on the grass.

She looked up and once again, the sky was like water she wanted to dive into. She had a bizarre, sudden memory from inside her swan body: of herself and her mother and father at the pool, of her sitting on her father's lap, the two of them watching as her mother walked out on the diving board, stretched her hands over her head, and dove into the water. The smell of tanning lotion and chlorine and melting candy. The three of them, together.

Then she ran, jumped, spread her wings and felt herself lifting up and up, just barely clearing the trees, and then, before she knew it, before she even had time to think about it, she was *flying*. Not just on the back of a bird now, she *was* the bird. Beautiful and whole and flying, with stars spinning and twirling above her, leaves swaying under her, the whole world unfolding in her path, opening up like there was a fire ripping through it. She went faster and faster. Higher! Ducking her head to miss the stars, diving down until she could see the tops of the chimneys of the little houses right in the center of town. There was her school! The university, its giant football stadium with the lit-up billboards outside. And then, past all that, more mountains, more trees, more winding swerving creeks and rivers.

She laughed and whooped, and the honking sounds that came out of her were lost in the wind.

This was her life! She wasn't dreaming!

She sped up even faster, relaxing her body into the air. Ecstatic.

And it occurred to her: This is what her mother had given up, to be with her father for the time that she was. Wasn't it? She gave up all of this to be in an earthbound, human body, and she'd even become pregnant in that body. Pregnant with Ava. Wouldn't she have felt so awkward and strange? Wouldn't she have *missed* this?

How wonderful it must have been, the first time her mother took again to the air!

Ignoring the pang of sadness that accompanied that thought, Ava swooped down and turned a circle in the air, twisting her long neck, tucking her feet up into her body.

The energy she had! She felt she could fly like this for

hours. Maybe she could visit New York! Or Alaska! She could probably go anywhere, couldn't she?

Woooooooo!

Tempting as it was, she was afraid of going *too* far this first time, just in case she got lost or ended up getting suddenly tired and going kaput in the middle of New Jersey. But it was *so nice*, being in the air. Not even the heat had any effect on her as she whipped through the wind, which was cool and perfect as it slid through her feathers.

There would be time for all of that, later.

So she turned in circles, dipped down, and flew over the treetops and houses, crossing the forest and passing over the creek, which looked like liquid silver—inviting and beautiful. She went across the valley they all lived in and then back again, criss-crossing it like the topping of an old-fashioned apple pie, the way Grandma Kay made it. When she passed over the forest again, tilting left and then right, even flipping over in the air, she was no longer even thinking about what she was doing. Just playing with the air and the sky and the stars. The stars spinning like tops, like toys spread out under a Christmas tree. And then, on a whim, she turned from the stars and just folded her wings and dove straight down, right into the water. Right in with the trout!

Ahhhh!

The water folded over her like the best, most comfortable blanket, or like the loveliest nap after a long day. She pushed forward, letting it envelop her, her wings tucked tight against her body. It felt so wonderful! She thought about the water at the lake, how she felt so alone and good when she was immersed in it—though the memories of her human body felt weirdly distant to her now—how free she felt, and then she rose to the water's surface, paddling her feet. Her body half in water and half in air. The air streaming through her wet feathers and the fish slipping under her. She laughed out loud, and her honking pierced into the quiet night.

How wonderful—to be back in the water, to be able to come here whenever she liked.

Then she launched herself up again, folding her legs and feet under her, and flew.

The world was so open to her!

She moved through the air, back and forth over town, until she suddenly recognized Grandma Kay's house under her. She dipped down and glided just over the dim streetlamps, past the line of houses with porches and rose bushes jutting out in front of them. She had flown right to her grandmother's house, without even thinking.

On impulse, she swooped down and landed on the lawn. It seemed so long since she'd seen her grandmother, though it had only been a few weeks before that Ava had stayed home sick from school and secretly paid her grandmother a visit. She laughed now, thinking of how freaked out she'd been—Ava, not her grandmother—that day. How awful it had been, having feathers pop out all over her body. And now look at her. Flying over the valley, turning circles in the air.

She laughed, honking.

A few minutes later the front door unlatched and her grandmother appeared on the porch, dressed in a light blue cotton robe. Ava stepped back, almost stumbling over. It had to be way past midnight—what was her grandmother even doing up?

Ava had thought she had the whole night, the whole valley, all to herself.

"Ava?"

Ava watched her grandmother in shock. Had she even heard her correctly?

Grandma Kay squinted into the night. "Ava, are you there?"

Ava caught herself, reached back and transformed into her human form again, so that she was standing on her grandmother's lawn in her pajamas, holding her feathered robe. "Grandma?"

"Oh, it is you! Come in, dear, what are you doing out there?"

"But . . ." Ava stammered, not sure what to say. So she kept quiet, folding the white robe in her arms, and headed up onto the porch and into the house.

Her grandmother reached out and touched her, smiling

and nodding her head as she patted Ava's arm. "Can I get you some cocoa, honey? Are you hungry?"

"No, I'm fine, Grandma."

"I baked some cookies this afternoon. Snickerdoodles."

"Oh. Well, okay, maybe one." Ava wasn't going to let a little weirdness come between her and her favorite cookies. Especially if Grandma Kay had made them.

"Then come help me get a tray together, and we can sit down and have a nice chat."

"Okay," Ava said, reaching out to help her grandmother down the hall.

Grandma Kay had a whole tin of Snickerdoodles sitting out on the counter, as if she'd been expecting Ava's visit, and there was a teapot of hot water on the stove.

"Were you ... Did you know I was coming?" Ava asked.

"Oh no." Her grandmother chuckled, waving her hand and taking out two mugs from the bright red cabinet. "I was just making myself some hot water with lemon." But she proceeded to pour two hot mugs of water, plunking a lemon slice in one and a bag of cocoa mix—the kind with marshmallows, which Ava loved—into the other.

Ava shook her head and placed the mugs and cookie tin onto one of the big silver trays on the counter, then followed her grandmother into the living room.

"So, honey," her grandmother said, settling into her rocking chair and tapping the coffee table, indicating where

Ava should set the tray, "tell me what's going on with you."

"Umm." She didn't know where to start, or what to start *with*. It was totally weird to be here like this with her grandmother acting like everything was normal. "A lot."

"Well, why don't we start with the swan maidens?"

Ava had just taken a huge bite of Snickerdoodle and immediately spit it out. Crumbs spewed over the table and over the carpet.

"Oh my!" her grandmother said. "Are you okay, dear?"

"Yes," Ava gasped, choking a little still. She coughed. There was cookie stuck in her throat.

"Take a sip of your cocoa."

Ava obeyed, letting the warm chocolate run over her tongue and down her throat. There was wet, chewed-up cookie on her nightshirt, she saw, and she plucked it off and set it on the table. "What did you say, Grandma?" she managed to get out.

"To take a sip of cocoa, dear."

"No *before* that."

"Oh, that we should start with the swan maidens."

"The swan…" Ava was too shocked to finish. She just stared at her sweet old grandmother, who was rocking innocently back and forth as if it were normal for her granddaughter to show up in her pajamas past midnight on a school night, as if there was nothing wrong at all with serving said granddaughter cocoa and casually asking her about swan maidens.

"They have come to you already, haven't they?"

"Yes."

Her grandmother nodded. "Good. It's about time. They couldn't before now, you know, so don't be upset with them."

"But . . . I don't understand. You know about them?"

"Yes, honey."

"You know about my mother?"

Grandma Kay sighed. "As soon as your father came home and told me he'd fallen in love with a swan maiden, I knew it would end up in tears and heartbreak. Swan maidens are not meant to mate with humans. Humans are not meant to mate with them." She sighed again, more heavily this time, as she reached for her lemon water and took a loud sip. "But he refused to listen to me. He was in love, he said. As if it were that simple." She shook her head. "I should have known it would happen, with the amount of time your father spent down at that creek."

"I can't believe you've known all this time, Grandma! Why didn't you tell me?"

She gave Ava a sad, concerned look. "You can't tell a child something like that. We had to wait until you were old enough for them to come to you themselves, so you could understand. How do you tell a three-year-old that her mother is a swan? We didn't want you to think your mother had left you on purpose. And what if we told you and then you left to find them and never came back? Think of your father. He is terrified you will leave him one day, too."

"But...my mother *did* leave me on purpose. Didn't she?"

"Oh honey, no. No no no. She loved you so much, Ava. She would have stayed with you and your father forever if she could have."

"Then why didn't she? And I can't believe... I thought he didn't know! Why... How could neither of you have told me the truth? About my mother, about me!" Ava burst into tears. One minute she was sitting there in shock, the next tears were streaming down her cheeks. Thank goodness her grandmother was nearly blind. Ava hated to cry in front of anyone, especially her evil secret-keeping grandmother. *She had known!!*

"Ava, Ava," her grandmother comforted, trying to hoist herself out of her rocking chair now.

"Stay there," Ava said. "Don't hurt yourself."

"Your grandfather told me I had to be careful, talking to you about this stuff. Oh, I wish he could tell you himself. I think your father was waiting for the full moon, to be sure. He's so scared, Ava. He worries so much about you. And then you got sick and everything . . ."

"Grandma, I don't understand anything you're saying! Why did my mother have to leave?"

Her grandmother took another sip of her water, and set it down. "Let me start at the beginning," she said. "You deserve to know all of this. You poor girl, you must be so confused."

"Yes!" Ava was sitting on the edge of the chair now. Waiting. "Hello! Of course I'm confused, thanks to you and Dad! Now please, Grandma, tell me what's going on!"

"Well, this, here, this valley," her grandmother began, "has always been a popular spot with swan maidens. Not everyone will admit that they're here, but why else do we have all these swans lurking around? Not everyone's seen a maiden that they knew of, and fewer still have seen one make the change . . . but"—she leaned forward—"my own great-grandmother used to tell me stories about them. And I always knew they weren't just stories."

Ava had plenty to say but forced herself to keep her mouth shut and let her grandmother talk, even if she was taking *far* longer than Ava would have liked. She couldn't beLIEVE her grandmother had known all of this, this whole time, and not said anything at all!!

"I never told your father those stories, though," she said. "I'm not sure why. I guess I didn't want to scare him, though maybe a little scaring would have done him some good, kept him out of those darn woods and away from that creek. But oh boy, as soon as your grandpa put a rod in your daddy's hand that first time, he was hooked." Ava's grandmother stopped and slapped her knee. "Hooked! Get it?"

"Grandma!"

"Okay, okay. So yes, your father has always been a fisherman. We do have the best trout fishing in the world right here, some say. But why the swan maidens had to come down the exact moment they did, I don't know. Plenty of the men around here have fished these waters their whole lives and never caught sight of one. But your father. Well, one evening he was out there all by his lonesome—he always was a little bit solitary, even as a young thing—when he looked up and saw three swans fall from the sky and to the side of that creek and turn into maidens right there smack dab in front of him." She shook her head, letting out yet another dramatic sigh. "What's a young man to do? He'd seen a miracle, and your mother might as well have thrown an arrow straight from her own hands and through to his heart. He told me all this later, of course, but I knew when he came home that day that something had happened to him. You could reach out and *smack* the spell that had come over him. Your grandfather didn't see it, of course, but I guess I've always been a little *touched*."

"So what happened? How did they end up together?"

"Well. Your father watched those swan maidens swimming, but really he had eyes only for your mother, not her friends. And he sat there watching them until they changed back and flew away."

"She left?"

"Yes, but he waited for her to come back. Waited and waited, with all the patience in the world, which love will give you, hiding behind a tree alongside the bank he knew the maidens would return to. And then they did."

"And then what?" Ava asked breathlessly.

"He stole her robe."

"He *what?*"

"He watched to see which robe was hers, and then he took it when they were in the water. When your mother and her friends emerged, her friends put on their robes and flew away, and your mother was stranded there."

Ava's mouth dropped open. How could he have done such a thing? Her sweet, goofy, handsome father!

"Don't judge him too harshly, Ava. He was in love, and love will make you crazy. It was the only way he could have been with her. And he would have given the robe back to her—he wouldn't have forced her to stay against her will—but she fell in love with him, too."

"But he tricked her!"

"Well, by the time she knew that, it was too late. And I doubt she would have cared. She was as crazy as he was! Some couples are like that, you know. Just madly, crazy in love with each other, no matter what. They don't care a thing for reason and have no sense at all."

"So she was just standing there, with no robe?"

"Yes. And he came out and took care of her, put his jacket around her and took her home. It was a full moon that night, of course. She was not meant to stay in human form any longer than that, but then she was trapped. But happy to be trapped, that's the thing. Your mother and father were very, very in love, Ava. And then they were married, and then they had you. I knew it couldn't end happily and I tried to warn him, but your father would have none of it."

"So what happened then? Why did she leave?"

"Oh honey. She grew ill. Your father took her to doctor after doctor, but no one could figure out what was wrong with her. She got thinner and thinner and took to her bed . . . Your father had to care for you, and I would come over and take care of you when he was off teaching, while your mother sat watching you, too weak to hold you—it made her so sad, not being able to hold you—and then one day your father brought out that robe, which he'd hidden away in the attic. He didn't realize what he was doing, he was just desperate for her to get better. And the moment he showed her that robe? Well, she had no choice but to put it on, and next thing your father knew your mother was a swan again, the way she'd been the very first time he saw her."

"She had no choice?"

"She was dying, Ava. She was not supposed to be a human. Swan maidens can change in the full moon, but that's it. They're meant to be swans."

"Is that . . ." A realization started to hit, and Ava felt like the whole world was shifting to its side and staying there. "Is that why he goes to the creek? On nights of the full moon?

Is he …"

"Yes," Grandma Kay said, her blue eyes glowing in the dim room. "He goes to see her."

Ava paused, thinking. "And so that day? She just turned into a swan and flew away?"

"Yes. The moment she put on that robe, she was herself again."

"He just let her go like that?"

"He had to, honey. She was never meant to stay. She stayed longer than she ever should have, and she would have stayed until she died if it had been up to her. Because of you."

"Because of me," Ava repeated.

She sat back, imagining all of it, feeling that warm moon inside her grow bigger and bigger. Her grandmother was tired now, she could see. She had been expecting her, hadn't she? Ava smiled as Grandma Kay's eyes fluttered shut, and then open again. It was so late! Ava herself would be exhausted the next day in school, and she had not one but two tests. They were easy ones, though, language arts and world history, and besides, what did tests matter now? There were only two days left of school, her birthday was in one week, and now she knew exactly what she was going to ask her father to give her. It would be the best birthday—and the best birthday present—ever.

As she flew home, her mind whirled with everything her grandmother had told her. She couldn't believe it, how beautiful and sad it all was—and that all the weird, freaky things that had been happening to her were all part of such a romantic story. Her cool, crazy dad, in love with a swan maiden, visiting with her mother under every full moon. At the same time, Ava felt such loss, thinking of all those nights that they sat together while she slept at home in bed, aching for a mother who was just minutes away.

Her mother! How terrible it must have been for her, to leave her husband and her child. And yet, she'd given up flight and her own beautiful world to be with them in the first place.

It was all so unfair!

And underneath it all, a thought niggled at Ava, a fear that started as a thin sliver and began to grow.

What if she, too, had to leave one day? Would she? Would she grow sick one day if she spent too much time in one world and not the other?

She remembered what Helen had said: "You can be one of them, and you can be one of us, too. Very few have the freedom to straddle two worlds. One day you will choose, but that is not for a long time yet." Is that what she had meant? And her grandmother, what had she said? That her father was terrified that Ava would leave him one day, too?

Ava's house appeared below her. She dropped down to

the edge of the woods behind it and reached back to pull off the robe, which came off in her hand.

If her mother's natural form was a swan, and staying in her human form for so long had made her sick ... could that happen to Ava one day, too?

Carrying her feathered robe, she stepped into the backyard.

"Ava?"

The voice startled her, seemed to come out of the night air. She froze.

Her eyes adjusted to the dark, her heart pounding. Had someone seen her transform?

She stood for a moment, listening, but the voice was silent.

Maybe she'd imagined it?

The robe in her arms was white and glittering. In a quick movement, she flung it behind her, back into the woods.

She took a deep breath and stepped forward. "Hello?" she whispered.

"What are you doing out here?" the voice said.

It was Jeff. Standing under the tree by her window, his cell phone in his hands. He looked up at the sky, and then back down at her.

CHAPTER ELEVEN

*T*he night was still, and the air warm, smelling of flowers and grass. Fireflies blinked in the air. In the distance, very faintly, someone was playing piano.

Ava stared at Jeff, unable to move. His face was half illuminated, half in the dark, but she saw his look of confusion.

What had he seen? She had been too distracted, too comfortable. And he had been standing right there, just steps away from where she was transforming! She had no idea if he could have seen her, from where he was standing.

He just stood staring at her, his face unreadable in the dark.

"I thought I saw..."

"Jeff!" she said, forcing herself to break into a big smile. Whatever he had seen, or hadn't seen, maybe she could trick him into thinking he hadn't seen anything at all.

She ran up to him and threw her arms around him. "Jeff! What are you doing here?" she said, pulling back and grinning up at him. She resisted the urge to look back and check to see that her robe was still there. "I'm so excited to see you!"

"You are?" His face broke into a shy smile, and she was pretty sure he was blushing.

"Yes! It is such a night for an adventure, isn't it? I was just taking a walk in the woods!"

She knew she was being a total dork, but she could be embarrassed about that later. Right now she just had to convince him that everything was normal.

"You were? By yourself, at night?"

"Of course!" she said, even though in truth she would never in a million years walk through the woods by herself at night. For one, they were chock-full of bugs. And now that she knew how weird everything was...for all she knew there could be werewolves back there, too.

His face shifted and he actually seemed impressed with her totally fictional adventurousness. "Cool," he said. "It was just strange, this big swan came flying down and a minute later you walked out! For a minute I thought you were carrying it."

"HAHAHA!" she laughed. "Carrying a swan . . . ?"

"Is there something you're not telling me?"

He was smiling, too, joking with her, but she got the impression he was suspicious and waiting to see what she would say.

She laughed again, even harder. "HAHAHAHAHAHA! I know! That thing almost knocked me over!!!!"

He laughed, too, and it seemed like he meant it, but of course she couldn't be sure.

"Swans are so impolite!" she continued. "HAHAHAH-HAHAA!"

She was acting like a crazy person, she realized, and suddenly stopped laughing. She cleared her throat. "So how are you?" she asked, widening her eyes, trying to give him an innocent this-is-all-totally-completely-and-utterly-normal look.

"Umm, good," he said, and she didn't know if she was imagining it or not, but he was looking at her very strangely. Of course, she *was* acting totally weird. But it seemed like he was looking at her in a I-just-saw-you-transform-from-a-swan-into-a-human-girl type way. "I came by earlier but you weren't here, so I was just stopping by on my way home."

"Oh!" She had forgotten how late it was. Which made it all the weirder for her to have supposedly been roaming around in the woods. "Did you go to the creek?"

"Yeah," he said. "The mayflies are gone now but it's so

beautiful this time of year, in the summer, especially when the moon is waxing. I was hoping you'd come with me."

Impulsively she grabbed his hand. What kind of boy talked about waxing moons? "That would have been nice," she said. "It's such a beautiful night, isn't it?"

And to her relief, he laced his fingers through hers. "Yeah," he said, smiling down at her.

She tried to enjoy the moment, but her heart was racing. It was making her crazy, thinking of her feathered robe, just tossed on the dirt.

She let out a huge fake yawn. "I'm so tired!" she said.

"Me too," he said, releasing her hand.

He had been about to kiss her, she realized, with a sinking heart. But if she didn't get her robe back, who knows what would happen? Surely she couldn't just grow another one anytime she wanted.

"So I'll see you at school tomorrow," he said.

"Can't wait!" she said brightly, like a huge dork, wanting to kick herself as he walked away.

Once he was out of sight, she raced back to the woods.

But the robe wasn't there.

Ava stared open-mouthed at the spot where she was sure she had tossed the robe. It couldn't have been more than ten minutes or so, could it have? She'd just reached back and tossed it, so Jeff wouldn't see. How could she have explained a huge glittering white-feathered robe practically breathing in her arms, as if she were holding a small animal? Would he have believed that she spent her night swan hunting and had nabbed one?

She stepped into the woods and tried to retrace her earlier movements, but after a few minutes stopped and turned back. She'd only been right at the edge of the woods, practically in the backyard.

Panic flowed through her.

Suddenly she felt ashamed and terrible, pretending like she was normal to Jeff and tossing her robe onto the ground as if it were a wrapper from McDonald's.

Not that she actually ever littered, she thought, choking back a sob.

And then, just as tears began streaming down her face, and a sense of loss overtook her, along with the sureness that she would never again fly and never know what the world of the swan maidens, and her mother, was really like, just as her heart was breaking into pieces, she saw something white and glowing on the ground, a few yards away.

It hadn't just been there a minute ago, had it?

She raced over, threw herself onto the ground, and gathered it up in her arms. The feathers seemed to move into her, like a cat.

She was so relieved! Though she was sure she hadn't thrown the robe that far and that it hadn't been there a minute ago ... but still. She had it back.

Suddenly there was a movement, a flash of white in the periphery. When she turned there was nothing there. She took a few steps in, stopped and listened, but whatever it was, if it had been anything at all, was gone.

Heading farther into the woods, she saw, on the ground, one gleaming white feather.

She waited another several minutes, listening to the rustling of leaves, the faint gurgling of the creek, and then, smiling to herself, she turned to go inside.

That night she dreamt about swans, but they weren't standing in the forest or swimming in the creek. They weren't flying above her as she lay in the backyard, or gathering outside her window.

Instead, in this dream, they were in another place, one she'd never before seen. There were fountains and waterfalls that sprayed mist into the air. The ground was soft with feathers, which sparkled underneath her bare feet.

Above her, sitting on a giant silver throne, was a beautiful lady with giant wings, looking down at her.

Ava reached for her, tried to step toward her, but her feet seemed to sink into the feathers and suddenly a thousand swans seemed to rise into the air in front of her, all at once.

At school the next morning, Morgan was waiting for her by her locker, even though Ava arrived halfway through the first period. She'd been sleeping so deeply she'd slept right through her alarm, which had gone off so long her father eventually had to come and shake her awake. Which had made him deeply cranky.

"Hey!" Morgan called.

"Hey. You're missing homeroom."

"Um, duh. So are you. What's wrong?" Morgan had her hands on her hips in her annoying Morgan fashion.

"What do you mean what's wrong?" Ava said, opening her locker.

Morgan rolled her eyes. "What do you mean what do I mean? Look at you! You totally look like you're gonna jump off a bridge."

"Oh, that's nice. I'm fine, I just barely slept."

"Why not?" Morgan demanded with her hands on her hips.

She was so bossy! Ava made a mental note to herself to make more friends.

"I put on the robe last night and flew, like, all over town, and I had these weird dreams after."

"You flew? Over the whole town? I didn't know that swans could fly like that!"

"Well, I can."

"That's like the coolest thing I've ever heard!"

"I know," she said. "And also. When I got home, Jeff was there. I think he might have . . . seen something." She felt sick as she remembered.

"He saw you . . . what, flying?"

"I flew home, and I was thinking about all this stuff and so I guess I wasn't really paying attention, and I transformed, in the back of the yard, almost in the woods. And he was there, Morgan, waiting for me, like he did before. I don't know what he saw, but he seemed really confused and suspicious, and I was definitely acting weird."

"Oh, well," Morgan said, waving her hand. "That's just normal, for you."

"Very funny."

Morgan batted her lashes. "So what happened?"

"Nothing, really. But Morgan, he had to have seen something, and if he didn't put it together last night, he will. He probably did when he got home. And if he did . . . I mean, what boy wants to date a swan?"

"Ummm, your dad?"

Ava shook her head. "My dad's different."

"So's Jeff," Morgan said softly.

"There's more to it, though. My grandmother told me all these things, like about my mom . . . and I don't know . . . I'm afraid I might be like my mom, I mean, more than I am now, even. Like maybe what happened to her will happen to me. You know?"

"Well, I don't know about that stuff, but being like your mom wouldn't be so bad anyway. *Right now*, though, you're a normal—well, semi-normal, let's be honest—girl, so you should quit worrying so much and just have fun being Jeff Jackson's girlfriend. Everyone's talking about the two of you. Wherever I go I hear people talking about you two."

"You do?"

"You haven't noticed?" Morgan rolled her eyes. "You're hopeless. You haven't noticed that everyone says hi to you and me now, too? Jennifer Halverson actually came up to me in gym class and complimented my sneakers."

"Those ugly things?"

"Yes! You see how extreme the situation is."

The bell rang then, signaling the end of first period.

"So stop being so weird. If Jeff saw anything, he'll get over it."

"That's easy for you to say! How do you know he won't find out and tell the whole school?"

"Well, look who it is," Morgan said, staring past Ava to someone down the hall, which was quickly filling up with students. "I guess he can tell us himself."

Ava moaned.

"Hey, Jeff!" Morgan shouted.

"Hey," his deep voice answered, right behind Ava.

She turned around, wincing.

But there he was looking normal and handsome and like

the most popular boy in school.

"Hey," she said, relaxing into a smile.

He leaned in, his blue eyes crackling in that weird, cool way. "How are you?"

"Tired," she said. "But happy."

"Me too. So do you want to go downtown with me after school?" he asked. "Maybe get some sno cones?"

"That would be great," she said, relief spreading through her whole body as Morgan made a gagging motion behind Jeff's perfect, golden blond head.

"Great," he said. "See you, Morgan!"

And then Ava turned to look at her friend's smug, but still sweet, face. "See?" Morgan said. "You have to stop being such a worrywart. He looooooves you."

Ava rolled her eyes and laughed.

Still, over the next few days, as she and her friends took their last tests and as school officially ended and the summer officially began, she couldn't stop thinking about Jeff Jackson's face in the moonlight, her robe glittering in the grass, and the beautiful lady sitting on that silver throne, just out of reach . . .

Who knew what the future would hold?

CHAPTER TWELVE

*S*ometimes it seems like a big day will never come. You wait and wait and count down the days, but time just slows down like sap dripping out of a tree, and you think you might go crazy watching that *drip...drip...drip* that stretches into eternity.

That is how Ava felt, at least, in the days leading up to her thirteenth birthday, even though school was out and it was summer in the middle of Pennsylvania, which is so beautiful with all those rolling hills and plunging ridges and bright green everywhere, on all sides of you, and all those pretty lakes laced with flowers and trees where your friends can hang out on sun-drenched afternoons as old-time carousels spin around and around like something inside a music box. Places like that are magical, whether or not the daughters of swan maidens come out to play. There were *swans*, though, all around, as Ava laid out at the lake or spent afternoons riding bikes or just hanging out in the backyard playing cards and listening to music with Jeff and Morgan (and Monique). They seemed to be everywhere these days, flying overhead or appearing for a moment in the periphery before disappearing again. As if they, too, were waiting and waiting for a day that might never come.

But the day did come, the way all such days eventually do, and Ava Lewis turned thirteen just as the moon grew as full and round and sparkling as a new coin.

That afternoon the heat let up a bit, and the whole valley seemed to let out a sigh of relief. Morgan came over right after lunch to help with the decorations, which she and Ava had bought on Ava's father's charge card, which he'd handed over to the girls the week before with a heavy, dramatic sigh.

Which seemed to run in the family.

Ava let one out now as she tried for the third time to tack up a glittery banner over the sliding doors. She and Morgan had taken pains to make *everything* as sparkling as possible. They even had cans of glitter to spray onto their skin and hair—and on Monique, who was later caught admiring herself in the glass door—and Ava had a new red dress with a dazzling sequined belt and a line of sequins around the hem. Jeff had offered to help, too, but Ava had told him absolutely not. She wanted him to come right at six p.m. like everyone else was going to, all dressed up and ready to celebrate in a house that had been magically transformed with paper and glitter and backyard tents filled with accordion-playing musicians.

If there was one thing Ava had learned about of late, it was magical transformations.

The house smelled amazing. Ava's dad was busy in the kitchen, cooking up a storm. The refrigerator was full, too, with Morgan's mother's concoctions that she'd sent over with Morgan in plastic bins. She herself would arrive at 5:30 to set up the cotton candy machine, which was her special gift for the event. "*Everyone* likes cotton candy," she'd said. "It puts everyone in a good mood."

The girls had certainly not argued.

And then, just after five, everything was ready. The house was lovely, inside and out. The backyard was full of picnic tables with umbrellas over them, and then tents for the food and the musicians. There was enough space for dancing, or just horsing around—Ava *had* invited all the boys in her grade, half of whom were incapable of acting like anything but hyped-up monkeys in a social setting—and for the cotton candy machine. And there were fairylights strewn over everything, along the sides of the house and stretching from umbrella to umbrella, that would light up as soon as it grew dark. Ava's father had even brought out some old tiki torches he'd stored in the basement that were now stuck in a few spots around the yard.

Ava and Morgan got ready together, sitting side by side, and took turns spraying each other with glitter and seeing if they could possibly look any cuter than they did.

Which, they both agreed, they couldn't possibly.

Ava couldn't wait for Jeff to arrive and see her in her new dress, on her birthday.

And then before they knew it, the doorbell rang, and didn't stop ringing until the backyard was full of soon-to-be eighth-graders.

And Jeff Jackson arrived, all dressed up in a nice shirt and tie, and five minutes later there was Josh Kirschner with his marble eyes, magically transforming Morgan from a clipboard-carrying taskmaster to a googly-eyed, giggling dork. Ava made sure to make many mental notes so as to torture her friend in the future, though for right now she was thrilled to see Morgan so happy. And if it all worked out, as it seemed it would, they could double date! With the two cutest—and nicest, as it turned out—boys in school!

Ava smiled just as Jeff came over and took her hand, leading her from the glass doorway onto the lawn, behind the tent where everyone was gathering to sample her dad's meatballs and Morgan's mother's famous artichoke dip.

Above them, a swan soared by, in the sky. Ava smiled up at it, and then looked right into Jeff Jackson's blue eyes.

He took her hand in his, and she could feel him trembling.

She swallowed. Shivers went up and down her spine.

Behind them their classmates were talking and laughing as the sun dropped slightly into the dip of the mountain, and her father's friends started tuning up. But she and Jeff Jackson were alone, in the midst of all the warmth and wonder.

"Ava," he said, his voice cracking.

She nodded, encouraging him. Her heart was pounding so loudly she was sure he could hear it. "Yes?"

"I think you're really . . . special. Different from other girls."

If only you knew how different, she thought. But she just smiled up at him, waiting.

"Like that night you were in the woods . . ."

"What night?" she asked, quickly.

"When you were holding that robe."

"Robe?"

"The one with the white feathers. I told you it looked like you were holding a swan, remember?"

She nodded, slowly. Did he know, after all? *Had* he seen her transform? He was giving her the strangest look.

"I just . . . It was amazing, Ava. Magical. Maybe one day you'll tell me more about it, what you do."

She didn't dare ask him what he meant, and hoped she was being paranoid.

"I feel lucky to know you," he said. "I feel like the luckiest guy in school."

"You do?"

He nodded, and his whole face softened, and she realized, suddenly, that he was going to kiss her, and that it didn't matter what he'd seen and what he hadn't seen, what he knew or didn't. Jeff Jackson was going to kiss her! Her face had to be the color of a tomato. Probably it was the exact same shade as her new dress.

Everything slowed down, but it was a good slowing down now, as he took a step closer to her and then bent down. She lifted her face and didn't dare to breathe.

"You're so pretty," he whispered.

"So are—" she began, and then his lips pressed into hers and without thinking her hands moved around his neck and his hands moved around her waist and they were kissing like that, and it was, she thought, the best moment of her entire life. Even better than flying.

And she would know.

The rest of the party passed in a blur of music and kissing and cotton candy and Jeff Jackson's arms around her and everyone whirling about in the grass—because once Ava and Jeff and Morgan and Josh started dancing to the old-people music, everyone else did, too, everyone but Jennifer Halverson and Vivienne Witmer, who sat sullenly in their seats with piles of meatballs in front of them—as Ava's dad laughed and played his banjo as if he hadn't a care in the world.

And before anyone knew it, the sun went down and the fairylights and torches came on, and everyone was barefoot on the grass in their button-down shirts and dresses, and parents and older brothers and sisters began showing up to take everyone home, and then even Jeff Jackson left, promising to come over the next day, and Josh Kirschner left, and Morgan's mother was packing up the cotton candy machine and helping Ava's father and his friends clean up and telling her daughter to get her bags, it was time to go home.

Morgan hugged her best friend good-bye and then looked at her with a big goofy expression, her green eyes filling with tears. "Have a beautiful night," she said.

"I will," Ava answered.

"I'm so happy for you."

"I'm happy for you, too. Josh really likes you."

"I know," Morgan said, so shyly and sweetly that Ava decided maybe she wouldn't torture her friend after all. Well, not *too* much. "Call me in the morning and tell me everything."

Ava nodded.

Morgan turned away and seemed to hesitate, and then she turned around again. "And come back, Ava. Don't you go away."

"I will," Ava whispered, smiling. "Don't be crazy."

"I guess I'm now officially allowed to be jealous, aren't I? Say hi to your mama for me."

And then it was just Ava and her dad standing happy and sleepy under the fairylights and the full moon and Ava's dad saying, "You still up for some fishing, kiddo? You look awfully tired," and Ava saying, "UMMM YES, what are we waiting for?"

"You might want to change out of that dress," Ava's father said, but Ava refused. Who cared if it was inappropriate to wear red dresses at the creek? It was her birthday and she wanted to look her best for whatever was about to take place.

"Lord help me, I'm the father of a teenager now," her father said, throwing up his hands and turning to the house. "From here on out, I'm picking my battles."

And as she stood in the yard waiting for her father to change his clothes and get the rods and lures and whatever other weird things they'd need—hopefully no disgusting bugs or beetles—Ava stared at the moon as she had so many times before, and all the stars surrounding it, and remembered what her grandmother had always told her: *You can see her, sometimes sitting on the moon, sometimes spread out over the stars, flying across the night sky.*

Just then, a few more swans passed overhead, and Ava realized that her grandmother had always told her something of the truth, in her way.

And then Ava and her father were making their way along the dirt path that led, windingly, down to the creek, and the moon shone down bright the way it had when Ava had walked this same path—or had it been a different one? a path she could only see with her swan eyes?—with the swan maiden Helen, and the water rushed by in front of them, gleaming and glittering in the moonlight, full of dazzled fish, and then Ava and her father were standing on the side of the creek and her father put the rod in her hand and said, "Like this. Flick your wrist back like this," but he seemed a little distracted, and kept looking up at the sky, and across the creek, and every little sound made him jump.

"Don't worry, Dad," Ava said softly, finally, taking pity on him. "She'll be here soon."

He looked at her as if he hadn't really seen her before that moment.

"Who?" he asked.

"Mama," she whispered, and as she watched his face change and shift, go from surprised to relieved to scared, she continued, "I am like her, you know. I have a robe now, too."

He breathed in and she realized: He was afraid she would leave him, the way her mother had. That she would leave him for the swan maidens.

"I thought it might be happening," he said, "that it would happen to you. I'm so sorry."

"Dad?" she interrupted him.

He looked at her. His eyes grew moist, gleaming in the moonlight.

"It's okay. I like being this way. Like Mama."

"You do?" Something like wonder passed over his face then, and it was as if her birthday happened all at once, right then and there, and she left her childhood behind. And she knew that no matter what happened in the future, everything would be okay.

"Yeah," she said. "I do. I like it. It's who I am."

He looked at her thoughtfully, nodding, and then he smiled. "She can't wait to meet you, you know. She's proud of you, Ava, and so am I."

She smiled back. And then she lifted the rod, bent her arm back, and flicked her wrist like he'd shown her: "Like this, right?"

"You're a natural," he said. "Now just skim it over the water. See how the lure sparkles? The fish get confused and think it's daylight. They're dazzled by it."

"Dazzled and moonstruck."

He tilted his head. "I suppose they are. But who isn't, really?" He threw out his own line, slowly reeled it in again.

They stood side by side, enjoying the silence, casting

their lines over and over again, letting the lures skim across the water.

After an hour or so, maybe more—it was hypnotic, Ava realized, no wonder her father could do this for hours and hours on end—a swan swooped down from the sky and landed on the side of the creek next to them.

Everything became still, and quiet.

The swan's feathers glittered under the moon, like fresh-fallen snow.

Ava watched the bird, transfixed, as her father wrapped his free hand around her own. She could sense his heart opening; and she didn't have to look up at him to see the dazzled look on his face. There had never been anyone else for him, not since the day he witnessed her mother and her friends swimming happily in the creek, their white feathered robes lying side by side along the shore.

Now, down farther, along the line of the water, more and more swans landed, entirely silent, so silent that if not for their soft, glowing forms Ava never would have realized they were there at all.

Watching them, Ava thought of how open the world would be to her from now on, all the adventures to come, all the dreams that would be explained, other worlds to explore . . . and it was as if the moon were her heart and it was all coming open, breaking open inside of her. The whole future spreading out in front of her like a great gift, full of water and sky, miracles and new worlds. What wonders there were in store!

The water lapped quietly. The moon shone bright and full overhead.

And then the swan in front of them began to transform, and Ava forgot everything else. Even knowing it was coming, she couldn't help but lose her breath as she watched the white feathers disappear, replaced by pale skin and a flowing white dress, the beak turning to lips, the long moon hair flowing down, and then her mother's face, her jewel eyes staring right at her. More beautiful, more perfect than Ava could have ever imagined.

Ava's father caught his breath beside her.

"Ava," her mother said, stretching out her pale, gleaming arm.

And in that moment, as she released her father's hand, Ava knew that no matter what happened in the future, what choices she'd have to make, who—or what—she would become, what would happen with Jeff, she would always be the daughter of two worlds . . . child of a father who fell in love with a swan maiden, child of a mother who fell in love with a human. She contained both worlds within her, with all their beauty and wonder and sadness, all the love that connected them, and that full, bursting moon that brought them together.

Ava released her father's hand, and stepped forward.

"Mama," she whispered. "You came."

THE END.